GW00535719

# DEATH
# by the
# Sea

Eliza Thomson Investigates

Book 7

By

VL McBeath

**Death by the Sea**
By VL McBeath

Editing services provided by Susan Cunningham
(www.perfectproseservices.com)
Cover design: BookCoversbyMelody
(https://bookcoversbymelody.com)

ISBNs:
978-1-913838-30-0 (Kindle Edition)
978-1-913838-31-7 (Paperback)

Main category - FICTION / Historical Mysteries
Other category - FICTION / Crime & Mystery

First Edition

Previous book in the
*Eliza Thomson Investigates*
series

*A Deadly Tonic* (A Novella)
*Murder in Moreton*
*Death of an Honourable Gent*
*Dying for a Garden Party*
*A Scottish Fling*
*The Palace Murder*
*A Christmas Murder* (A Novella)

**Get your FREE copy of *A Deadly Tonic*.**

Sign up to a no-spam newsletter for further information visit
https://www.subscribepage.com/eti-freeadt

Further details can be found at **www.vlmcbeath.com**

## CHAPTER ONE

*July 1905*

E liza Thomson linked the arm of her companion, Connie Appleton, as they descended the final flight of marble steps of the grand staircase in the Metropole Hotel, Brighton. She waved to her husband, Archie, as he waited for them in the foyer with her father, Mr Bell. His Scottish lilt sounded out of place as he called to them.

"About time, too. What have you been doing?"

"Settling ourselves in, obviously. There's an etiquette to be followed when one stays in such a smart hotel, and taking afternoon tea in the clothes one has travelled in isn't part of it." She ran her eyes over the guests milling around them. "Not that we've kept you for long. I doubt you've even had time to see the sea yet."

"We most certainly have, and it looks wonderful. There are men with their trouser legs rolled up, paddling at the water's edge, and women trying to stop the children from getting their clothes wet."

Mr Bell interrupted. "Don't forget those who were in the sea up to their necks. They seem to be having a marvellous time."

Eliza shuddered. "Well, don't expect me to do that. I've no intention of changing on the beach. Even in this weather."

Archie laughed. "If you're shy, they have bathing machines where you can change while they take you out to sea."

"That doesn't sound easy."

"I don't see why not, especially when it means you can descend the steps straight into the water. No one will see you and there are women called dippers who will help, and even push you under the waves. It's supposed to do you the world of good. I'm going to give it a try."

"Now?"

"Don't be silly. I've arranged a table for afternoon tea before we go out for a walk. I didn't think there'd be any free, the time we've waited for you. Besides, the tide's on its way out. I suspect we'll be better going in the early morning while the water's higher up the beach."

"When normal people should be in bed, by the sound of it."

Connie giggled. "Don't worry, I'll still join you for breakfast. I don't want to get wet, either."

"I'm glad to hear it." Eliza patted Connie's hand. "Now, where's this table?"

"This way, madam." Archie gave a bow as he escorted them towards a grand arch on the right-hand side of the lobby that led to the lounge. "I asked for a seat by the window."

"That will be nice. Then I can see what all the fuss is about."

"Didn't you take a look from the bedroom?"

"I've not had time." Eliza huffed as Archie shook his head.

"It's actually a better view from up there. You can't see the beach from here because it's a lot lower than the road. You can see the sea, though."

As they entered the large, opulent space, Eliza gazed at the wall of arched windows that looked out over the promenade. "It certainly looks lovely, with the sun glistening on the waves. I hope the weather holds for the week."

The maitre d' showed them to a table set between two palms, and Eliza was about to sit down when a short, dark-haired waitress joined them.

"Good afternoon." The girl's blue eyes glistened as she smiled. "Have you just arrived?"

"About an hour ago." Archie took a seat next to Eliza.

"Well, you sit there and relax. My name's Mrs Dunn and I serve the tables in this part of the lounge ... unless you specifically want a waiter..."

Eliza smiled at her. "We're perfectly happy for you to serve if you can bring us afternoon tea. We've spent most of the day on the train."

"You're from London, are you?"

"From the outskirts, so we needed to get to London before changing trains."

"At least you could do that. I used to walk everywhere when I lived there. I've only been on one train, and that was when I moved here. Everything's much closer together in Brighton. More relaxed, too."

"Which part of London are you from?"

"Lambeth, near the river. Not that it compares to being near the sea."

"I doubt anywhere in London is quite like this."

"So, you're on holiday?"

Eliza smiled. "We are. And it feels like an age since luncheon."

The girl laughed. "I'm sure it does. The sea air down here makes you hungry, too. Don't ask me why…" She paused as Eliza glanced at the teapot on a nearby table. "Right. Afternoon tea for four. I won't be long." She put her notebook in the pocket of the starched white apron that covered the front of her black dress and scurried away as Eliza settled back in her chair.

"Nice girl, but I've a feeling she likes to talk. I was worried we'd have to wait another half an hour."

Mr Bell pointed over Eliza's shoulder. "You still might. She's stopped to speak to someone else."

Eliza turned towards a table occupied by an older woman. "Urgh, no … oh, it's all right, she's moving again." She studied the rest of the room with its full-length curtains and ornately decorated ceiling. "It's very nice here. I thought the reports in the newspaper about how smart the hotel is, must have been exaggerated, but I don't think they were."

Mr Bell grinned at her. "Would I have brought you here if I thought you wouldn't like it?"

"No, you wouldn't, and thank you. It's most generous of you."

"Yes, thank you, Mr Bell." Connie sighed, causing Eliza to turn towards her.

"What's the matter? Aren't you happy?"

"Oh, I am, very, but I was thinking what a shame it is that Frank, I mean Sergeant Cooper, couldn't join us."

"He'll be here on Tuesday. It's better than nothing."

"It is, but I wish they didn't make him work so hard. I don't know that he'd ever be able to take a full week off like Dr Thomson."

"If I can find someone to do my job, I'm sure Sergeant Cooper can. Isn't Constable Jenkins ready to move into a sergeant's role? Maybe he could stand in."

Connie shuddered. "Sergeant Cooper wouldn't like that. He'd worry he'd have no job when he got back."

"Surely it wouldn't come to that..." Archie stopped and swivelled in his chair as a voice called out to him.

"Archie Thomson?"

He stood up and strode across the room towards a tall, dark-haired man heading his way. "Good gracious. David Shaw. Fancy seeing you."

"Fancy, indeed. Are you staying here?"

"Yes, we've not long since arrived. What about you?"

"The same. I've left my luggage with one of the porters to take upstairs while I search out a cup of tea. I didn't want to waste any energy climbing the stairs when there was no need."

"No change there, then." Archie chuckled as he ushered the man to their table. "You remember my wife? Miss Bell, as was."

He gave a crooked smile. "As if I could forget. It's been a long time."

Eliza offered him a hand. "Nearly twenty years, I would say."

"Is it really? Well, you haven't changed a bit." He smiled at Connie. "And who have we here?"

Archie offered his friend a chair. "This is Mrs Appleton, my wife's companion, and this..." he indicated to Mr Bell "...is Eliza's father. Mr Bell, this is an old friend of mine, Dr David Shaw."

"Pleased to meet you." Mr Bell extended a hand before retaking his seat. "Are you down here on holiday?"

"Not exactly, although it will feel like one after being in London." He opened his arms to the window. "Have you seen the sea? Doesn't it look inviting? Just the thing to relieve the nerves."

Archie laughed. "You don't suffer with nerves, surely..."

"You've no idea... The work in London was driving me mad..." He stopped as the waitress appeared beside him, a large tray in her hands. She hesitated as her eyes fell on Dr Shaw.

"You didn't say you were having visitors. I've only brought enough for four."

Dr Shaw looked up with a smirk. "Bring another cup and saucer ... and plate ... there's a dear. Dr and Mrs Thomson didn't know I was joining them. Neither did I, for that matter." He laughed as she pursed her lips.

"Yes, sir."

Mr Bell sat forward in his seat. "How do you all know each other?"

Eliza glanced between them. "Archie and Dr Shaw were at medical school together. I met Dr Shaw at one of the university balls and he ended up introducing me to Archie."

Dr Shaw laughed. "Did I really? I'd forgotten about that."

Eliza shook her head at Archie. "Don't tell me you'd forgotten, too."

"As if I would."

"I should hope not." Eliza studied Dr Shaw. "Did you ever marry?"

"Never found the time for it, to be honest. The work in these hospitals never stops."

"You must enjoy it or you wouldn't stay."

"I'm not staying, thank goodness. I handed in my notice of intent to leave St Thomas's Hospital a week ago, finished yesterday, and I start a new role down here on Monday."

"That was quick. Had it been in the planning?"

"No, not at all. I just woke up one morning and decided I'd had enough. So here I am. It should make life easier." He turned to Connie. "I specialise in children's medicine and I've had quite enough of the parents in London. I expect they'll be a lot more compliant and less demanding down here."

The waitress had returned silently to the table and set down the additional crockery. "Will that be all?"

"I think so, thank you." Eliza smiled at her. "We'll call if we need anything else." She handed plates to each of them. "This all looks rather nice. Shall we start?"

Dr Shaw took a selection of sandwiches as he spoke to Archie. "Are you still in London?"

"No, I left about four years ago. I run a surgery in a small village near Hampton Court Palace now. I'm amazed I've not seen you since."

Dr Shaw shook his head. "You can't have done, I'm sure I'd have remembered. It explains why we've not bumped into each other recently, though. I presume you're here on holiday."

7

"We are." Archie nodded to his father-in-law. "Mr Bell has kindly treated us for our wedding anniversary. Twenty-two years."

Dr Shaw let out a low whistle. "That makes me feel old. I'm only staying here because the hospital's paying until I find somewhere to live."

"You'll be in no hurry to start looking, then."

Dr Shaw grimaced. "I've got a week. That's all they'll pay for."

Archie accepted the cup of tea Eliza passed to him. "You better make the most of it, then."

"I'll certainly try." He grinned at Connie, but her eyes narrowed, and she sat up straight.

"My gentleman friend is joining us shortly."

Dr Shaw turned in his chair. "Have we started without him?"

"No." Connie raised her chin. "He's a police officer and they couldn't manage without him for a week."

"That's a shame. When he arrives, tell him to try the water. It's very refreshing. I'll be going in first thing tomorrow morning. What about you, Archie? Will you join me?"

Archie glanced at Eliza. "Not tomorrow. I still need to persuade Eliza it's a good idea. Perhaps later in the week."

"I'll hold you to it."

"As long as you don't expect me to join you." Eliza lowered her gaze as she checked the teapot. "We could do with some hot water to top this up. Let me see if I can catch the waitress's eye." She waved an arm. "That's a nuisance, she's talking to that woman again..."

Dr Shaw finished his tea and pushed himself up from his chair. "Don't get any more on my account. I need to check my bags have arrived in the right room. I'm going out for dinner tonight, so can't be late. Hopefully, I'll see you when I get back, but if not, enjoy your evening."

Archie and Mr Bell stood up as he left, but Connie shuddered. "He had me worried for a minute."

Eliza patted her hand. "There's no need. He's harmless enough and now he knows about Sergeant Cooper he won't trouble you."

"I hope you're right."

Archie smiled at her. "I'll have a word with him if you like."

"Please don't make a fuss…"

Eliza raised an arm to the waitress once more. "Ah, she's seen me." She waited for her to join them. "Might we have a jug of hot water to top up the teapot, please?"

"Is it for the four of you, or will the other *gentleman* be returning?"

"Just for four. He's gone for now, thank you."

The smile returned to the woman's face. "Give me a minute, and I'll be back. It's been one of those afternoons."

# CHAPTER TWO

The air was still warm when they left the hotel to walk along the promenade, and by the time they turned to make their way back, the sun was behind them. As they approached, Eliza stopped to study the beach.

"It really is a lovely place. And you're right about the people looking as if they're enjoying themselves ... even with the tide being so far away."

"Does that mean you'll sit on a deckchair with us tomorrow?"

Eliza grinned. "Perhaps. As long as we can find some shade to sit in. It will be too hot otherwise."

"That's why folks go into the sea, to cool down. I'm telling you, you should try it. There are some bathing costumes in the hotel shop, if you're interested."

Eliza rolled her eyes. "Don't get carried away. You go in the water if you like, just don't involve me or Connie."

"Very well. Mr Bell and I will go without you. I'll make arrangements with David for Monday morning." He checked his pocket watch. "We've another half an hour before dinner. Shall we have a pre-dinner drink?"

Eliza's face lit up. "That sounds more like it. Lead the way."

The doorman tipped his hat to them as they went inside, but as Archie approached the centre of the foyer he turned in a full circle, attracting the attention of a stoutly built porter.

"May I help, sir?"

"We're hoping to have a sherry before dinner. Is there a place the ladies may join us?"

"Certainly, sir." The young man strode towards the lounge. "Ladies are always welcome in here. If you take a seat, one of the waitresses will serve you shortly. If you gentlemen would care for a brandy and cigar after dinner, the smoking room is through the next arch along, behind the bar."

"Thank you..." Archie studied the man's name badge "... Mr Dunn."

"Not at all."

"Are you related to the lady who served us earlier? Mrs Dunn?"

Mr Dunn smoothed a hand over his moustache. "She's my wife. She likes to work, to keep herself busy. I know it's not usual..."

Eliza rested a hand on his arm as he fidgeted with his fingers. "There's no need to explain. I work with my husband, too. It's becoming popular."

"Ah, yes. Yes, it is." Colour rose in his cheeks. "Well ... enjoy your evening."

Eliza smiled as they strolled into the lounge. "How quaint that he was embarrassed about his wife serving. It's time men accepted wives are capable of working."

Mr Bell huffed. "I assumed she was a widow when she first introduced herself."

"That's because she would have been when you were younger. We're in new times now." She glanced out of the window as they approached the table they'd sat at earlier. "At least you get a pleasant view sitting in here. You won't get as good a view in the bar."

Archie raised an eyebrow at Mr Bell. "Perhaps we'll find out later. Oh..." He stopped and pointed at a head resting on the back of one of the wing-back chairs. "Someone's beaten us to it." He was about to turn away when Dr Shaw stood up.

"Is that you, Archie?"

"David, yes. I'm sorry to disturb you. I didn't think anyone was sitting here."

"And they won't be in a minute. I'm about to leave."

"Are you on your own?"

"I came in for a quick drink before I go out." He drained the last of his cocktail. "I've arranged to meet an old acquaintance at a restaurant in the town centre."

"That's a shame. You'll miss out on eating here."

"It's only for tonight. It's someone I used to work with who moved down here. I'm hoping they'll help me find somewhere to live, so I suggested we meet up ... before I knew how smart this place was, obviously." He rolled his eyes. "Anyway, I'll be here for the rest of the week. If you're around when I get back this evening, I'll join you for a drink."

"I expect we will be, assuming you're not too late. Will you be in here or in the bar?"

He grinned. "Anywhere they'll serve me. I'll look out for you when I arrive. I'll see you later."

Archie watched him go. "Same old David. It's as if we only saw each other last week."

"You have seen him on occasion when you've been in London."

"I have, but never for long. Hopefully, we'll have chance for a proper catch up this week. Assuming he's not too busy looking for somewhere to live."

"Even if he is, he won't be of an evening."

"The best time to socialise..."

Mr Bell nodded. "He seemed rather full of life. I hope he doesn't keep you up too late tonight. I may have to leave you to it."

"You needn't worry. I expect he's just excited about being here. It's a big move from London, and it's not many doctors' salaries that can afford to stay at a place like this. They must have wanted him at the hospital."

"Well, good for him." Eliza took a seat beside Connie and cocked her head to one side. "I wonder what happened to that girl he was walking out with when we were married. I thought they'd be next down the aisle, but clearly not."

"I'll ask him later, assuming he's still coherent." Archie sniffed the empty glass. "Some sort of vermouth cocktail, I'd suggest."

Eliza creased her cheek. "It's to be hoped he doesn't have many of them."

Archie laughed. "You're right. I think we'll stick to sherry."

Archie hadn't put the glass down before a waitress appeared by his side. "Let me take that, sir. I'm sorry the table wasn't ready for you."

"Not at all. The previous guest was still here when we arrived."

"Has he left?" The woman, whose dark hair was fastened at the nape of her neck, glanced around.

"Yes, he's gone out for dinner, so it's just the four of us."

"And what may I get you?"

"Four sweet sherries, please."

"Very good, sir."

Eliza shifted in her seat. "Is everything all right with Mrs Dunn?"

The waitress's forehead furrowed as she stared at her. "Mrs Dunn? Yes, she's fine. Why?"

"Oh, no reason, other than she told us earlier that she usually serves these tables."

"Oh, that." The waitress chuckled. "She's working at the other end of the room tonight. We sometimes change to relieve the boredom. Not that we get bored with the guests, you understand..." Her cheeks coloured. "I-I meant..."

Eliza smiled. "I know what you meant. It just gives you a change of scenery."

"Yes, that's exactly it. Thank you. I'm Miss Anderson, in case you were wondering."

"It's nice to meet you, Miss Anderson." Eliza thought the girl was about to curtsey, but after a brief hesitation, she put her notebook in her pocket and dodged around a series of tables as she headed for a door on the far side of the room. She was almost there when she stopped and waited for Mrs Dunn to join her. Eliza nodded in their direction.

"They seem friendly."

"I suppose you have to be if you're working together all day, every day. You said yourself, Mrs Dunn likes to chat."

"I did, but looking at her now, she's not as bubbly as she was earlier. I hope we've not upset her."

"Why would we?" Connie scowled. "She did say it had been one of those days. Maybe she has other things on her mind."

"I suppose so. It can't be easy working if you're distracted."

Archie glanced over his shoulder. "As long as it doesn't slow her down. It will be time to eat before we get this sherry."

The dining room was situated across the foyer from the lounge, and after a dinner of poached chicken and mashed potato, Eliza sat straight in her chair and dabbed her lips with her napkin.

"That was lovely."

Mr Bell eyed her plate. "I hope you've left room for dessert. They have apple pie and custard on the menu."

Eliza chuckled. "I thought you'd spot that, but I'm more tempted by the rice pudding. It's not so filling."

"I'll always finish your apple pie if you need any help."

"I'll stick to the rice pudding if you don't mind." She turned to Connie. "Will Sergeant Cooper be able to stay for dinner when he comes on Tuesday?"

"I don't know yet, but I doubt it. It's nearly eight o'clock already and we've not had dessert yet. He wouldn't make the last train to Moreton."

"We could always eat a little earlier." Eliza looked at Archie. "That would be all right, wouldn't it?"

"I don't see why not. Although it may mean we have to spend more time in the bar afterwards."

"You can go for one drink and then sit with us in the lounge. We're supposed to be on holiday together."

Mr Bell patted her hand. "And so we are, but I'm sure you and Mrs Appleton would be quite happy to be on your own every now and again."

Eliza pursed her lips. "All I'm saying is, don't make a habit of it. Not that I have any objection about tonight. I'm quite exhausted after such a busy day and think having an early night would be a good idea. Would you mind if I did?" She looked at Connie.

"Not at all. I was hoping not to stay up late myself. The waitress we spoke to earlier may have said the sea air makes you hungry. I think it makes you tired, too."

"We'll send your apologies to David, then." Archie looked at Mr Bell. "I'm sure we can manage on our own."

"I expect so."

Eliza tutted. "Given you agreed to meet him for a drink, possibly in the bar, I doubt he'll be expecting us, anyway. Tell him we'll see him tomorrow."

# CHAPTER THREE

The following morning, Eliza gazed down at the plates of scrambled eggs the waitress placed in front of her and Connie before she looked up with a smile. "Thank you. That looks lovely."

Archie sniffed the air. "These kippers smell good, too."

She picked up her knife and fork. "Did you stay up long with David last night? I was fast asleep when you came to bed."

"Thankfully, we weren't as late as I feared. We were still in the lounge when he found us, but he said he had an upset stomach and decided to have an early night himself. Not that it was particularly early in the end..."

Eliza creased her cheek. "Had he eaten too much when he was out?"

"He wasn't sure, but he had a couple of large brandies to sort it out and then walked upstairs with us at about half past eleven."

"That's unfortunate. He must have wished he'd stayed in the hotel."

"He didn't say, but he seemed to have had a nice evening."

"Well, hopefully we'll see him later. He was keen to go into the sea this morning. I hope he made it."

Archie glanced out of the window to his right. "I'm sure he will have done. He said he'd tell me about it over luncheon." He turned back to Eliza. "Are we going to church later?"

She set down her knife and fork. "I hadn't planned on it. Does anyone want to go?"

Mr Bell took a bite of bread and butter. "I'm sure it wouldn't matter if we missed it for a week. I'm not even sure where we'd go."

"Me neither. The only church I saw on the drive from the railway station was Catholic. Shall we go for a walk this morning instead? We could go in the opposite direction to the way we walked yesterday."

"That would be nice." Connie sat back in her chair. "I'd like to see more of the place before Sergeant Cooper joins us. I'm sure he'll want me to show him around."

"That's settled then." Eliza grinned at Archie as she returned to her breakfast. "And if we go for a walk this morning, perhaps we can sit on the beach this afternoon."

He laughed. "The sea air has clearly gone to your head."


Eliza moved her parasol from one shoulder to the other as they left the pier and turned left towards the hotel.

"We'll have to come here again. There's so much to do. It would even be nice to sit in the reading room with a newspaper if the weather takes a turn for the worse."

"We could do that. I'd like to try out the amusement machines, too."

"I'm sure you would." She studied the length of beach below them, squinting at a small group of people around a bathing machine opposite the hotel. "Do you see that over there? Is it the police?"

Archie followed her gaze. "It certainly looks like it."

"We'd better get a move on."

Archie scowled at her. "Why?"

"So we can find out what's going on."

"There's no need. It's none of our business."

Eliza tutted at Connie. "Will he ever learn?"

Connie giggled. "Why don't we walk along the beach, so it appears more natural when we arrive?"

"That's a good idea." Eliza stared at Archie as he tutted. "You've wanted us to visit the beach since we arrived, and now we suggest it..."

"All right. If you must."

Eliza quickened her pace, skipping down the first flight of steps they saw, but stopped when she landed on the pebbles. "These won't be easy to walk on."

Archie took her arm. "What did you expect? Can you manage, Mrs Appleton?"

Before she could answer, Mr Bell offered to help. "Let me."

"Thank you. It is more difficult than it looks, especially with the heels on these boots."

"Exactly!" Eliza huffed as they trudged towards the bathing machine. "I knew there was a reason I didn't want to come down here."

"There are more steps coming up. You can always go back to the promenade."

"I'll manage, thank you. We're nearly there."

Perspiration covered Eliza's forehead by the time they reached the bathing machine, but before they could see what was happening, a police officer ushered them to the left towards the sea.

"Walk around the barriers, please. There's nothing to see here."

Eliza stayed where she was, her eyes fixed on the door of the cabin. "My husband's a doctor. If someone's ill..."

A short, bearded man, with grey hair visible around the rim of his hat, appeared from inside the machine and waved to the policeman in charge. "I'll arrange for someone to come and pick him up as soon as they can, and I'll call into the station once I've done the post mortem."

"Right you are, Dr Poole."

"Ask him what's going on." Eliza pushed Archie forward, causing him to stumble.

"Oh, excuse me. My wife..." He glared at her, but she ignored him as she addressed the doctor.

"It sounds like you have an unpleasant job on your hands."

The man straightened his jacket. "You'll need to ask Inspector Jarvis about that."

"Oh, we will, but if we can help..." Eliza kicked Archie's foot.

"Yes, right..." Archie extended his hand. "Dr Archie

Thomson. I presume you're the doctor who certified the death. Do you know the identity of the body?"

The man stared at him before accepting his handshake. "Dr Poole. How do you know there's a body?"

"You said you'll call into the station once you've done the post mortem..."

"Ah. I should keep my voice down." The doctor huffed and looked back at the bathing machine. "It's a sad state of affairs. It looks like the fellow drowned, but other than finding a book of matches from the Metropole in his pocket, we've no idea who he is. We'll have to get someone from the hotel to see if they recognise him."

Archie raised an eyebrow. "The Metropole? My wife and I are staying there. Perhaps I could help."

The doctor glanced at the police officer. "I'd happily let you take a look, but I'd better clear it with the inspector first."

Archie waited as the doctor spoke to the officers, and once the formalities were over, Eliza, Connie and Mr Bell waited by the barrier while the inspector escorted Archie and Dr Poole to the bathing machine. It felt like an age before he reappeared, his face ashen.

Eliza's eyes widened. "What's the matter?"

The officer appeared to ignore her, but Archie ushered them over.

"It's David."

Eliza's stomach sank. "Dead?"

He nodded.

"And he drowned?"

"It would appear so."

Eliza's forehead creased. "Could it have had anything to do with his upset stomach?"

21

The inspector sneered at her. "I hardly think a stomach ache is likely to cause drowning."

"It might..."

Archie gave the officer an apologetic smile before addressing Eliza. "Dr Poole says one of the dippers found his body at around ten o'clock this morning when she came to prepare the bathing machines for the day."

Eliza studied the beach. "But the tide's out. How could he have drowned if he only came here this morning?"

Dr Poole interrupted. "Don't let it worry you, madam. The police will deal with it. Now, if you'll excuse me."

"But you must tell us. Please. My husband was with Dr Shaw last night. We need to know what happened."

Archie sighed as he addressed the doctor and Inspector Jarvis. "If you wouldn't mind. My wife has a peculiar interest in such matters, so it would make my life easier."

Dr Poole nodded. "Very well. Based on the tidal times and the near complete onset of rigor mortis, we believe he died somewhere between midnight and three o'clock last night."

"B-but..." She looked at Archie. "You said he went to bed at the same time as you. Why would he be on the beach?"

Archie shrugged. "I've no idea."

Dr Poole raised his hat to them. "I'm sure the police will work it out. Now, I really must go."

The inspector's eyes narrowed as Dr Poole left them. "You were with the deceased last evening?"

"Not for the whole time." Archie straightened his back. "He'd been out to a restaurant in town and joined myself and my father-in-law in the lounge of the Metropole when he returned." He beckoned Mr Bell forward. "Inspector Jarvis, Mr Bell."

The two shook hands as the inspector looked him up and down. "So you were together all evening."

"We were. My daughter and her companion left us at about nine thirty and we stayed in the lounge." Mr Bell turned to Archie. "I'd say Dr Shaw joined us at about a quarter past ten and we were there for another hour or so."

Archie nodded. "That about sums it up. He said he felt under the weather when he came in and had two large brandies while we were with him. We all went to bed somewhere between quarter past and half past eleven."

The inspector turned to Eliza. "And you can confirm that?"

"I... Well... No, actually I was asleep when my husband came upstairs."

The inspector nodded as he wrote in his notebook. "What about you, Mr Bell? Can anyone confirm your whereabouts?"

"Not unless one of the waiting staff or porters noticed us leave. I have a single room."

"We'll be speaking to all the staff over the next day or two, but I must ask you not to leave the hotel until we've finished our enquiries."

Eliza spluttered. "You can't think they had anything to do with David's death?"

"We need to keep an open mind, Mrs Thomson. Now, if you can make yourselves available in the hotel this afternoon, I'll come and take formal statements from you."

Eliza glared at the inspector as he wandered to his constable. "What a cheek. You help him out like that and he thinks you're a suspect..."

"He thinks nothing of the sort. He just needs to take a

statement from us. It's all your fault, anyway. I told you not to get involved..."

"Don't blame me." Seeing the inspector still had his back to her, Eliza slipped around the barrier. "Give me a minute..."

"What are you doing?" Archie spoke through gritted teeth. "You'll get us all into trouble..."

"I won't if you don't say anything." She beckoned Connie to follow her to the bathing machine, thankful someone had covered David's body with a sheet.

"Look at this. The water mark isn't very high, but it would be enough to cover his face."

"Not by much."

"That doesn't matter. If he couldn't sit up, he'd have drowned in any depth of water. Surely he must have realised the tide was coming in."

Connie put a hand over her nose as she peered inside. "Could he have been too ill to move?"

"Perhaps, but how did he get here if he was so ill? The bathing machine is a long way down the beach." She let out a deep sigh as she glanced from the promenade to the sea, but suddenly grabbed Connie's arm. "We'd better go ... quickly." They hadn't reached the barrier before Inspector Jarvis stood beside them.

"What were you doing poking around in there?"

"N-nothing. We're going." Eliza pushed Connie through the gap in the barricade.

"Have you touched anything?"

"Of course not. I just wanted to check on something."

"There's nothing for you to check."

Eliza huffed. "If you must know, I wanted to see how far up the machine the water had come."

"That's of no concern to you. Now I suggest you leave before I have you arrested."

Eliza was about to respond when Archie caught hold of her arm.

"Leave it."

The inspector glared at them. "I suggest you all leave. I'll be in touch this afternoon to find out what you're really up to."

Archie waited for the inspector to go back to the bathing machine. "Now look what you've done. What were you doing?"

"Finding evidence the doctor and police obviously missed."

"What evidence?"

"Didn't you notice the smell? I would say that David was very ill while he was in there. Given he ended up on the beach on the same night he had a stomach ache, it makes me wonder if there's more to this than meets the eye."

# CHAPTER FOUR

S unlight filled the expansive dining room as Archie ushered them to their table for luncheon. Miss Anderson pulled a heavy velvet curtain across the left-hand side of one of the large arched windows that ran the length of the wall.

"There we are. That should keep the sun from your eyes."

"Thank you. It's such a shame to hide the view, but I suppose we need to see what we're eating." Eliza smiled as she took her seat beside Connie. "We shouldn't complain about the weather, but it is rather warm out there."

"I'm sure it is. It's hot enough in here. Will it just be the four of you for luncheon or will your friend be joining you? He always seems to arrive once you've placed your order."

Archie smiled at her. "It's just the four of us. Thank you."

"Yes, unfortunately, we won't be seeing him today. Oh..." Eliza winced as Archie kicked her foot. "It looks like you're busy. Is that why you're in the dining room rather than the lounge?"

"I'll move over there this afternoon. We work where we're

needed, and everywhere else is usually quiet while luncheon's being served."

"I'm not surprised. I wouldn't want to miss it."

Miss Anderson grinned. "Will you have our dish of the day? Roast beef, roast potatoes, vegetables and Yorkshire pudding."

"Certainly I will. It wouldn't be Sunday otherwise."

"That's what I always say. What about everyone else?"

Following a succession of nods, the waitress looked up from her notepad. "And what would you like to drink? We have some lovely elderflower cordial. Or a jug of freshly made lemonade?"

Eliza checked around the table. "Lemonade, please. We've worked up quite a thirst this morning."

The waitress gazed out of the window. "I heard there was a bit of a commotion outside earlier. Did you see what was going on?"

Eliza opened her mouth to speak, but Archie interrupted.

"Not really. The police had roped off a section of the beach to keep people away. I'm sure they'll be in to tell us what it's about if they need to."

"Well, I hope they wait until after luncheon. I'm busy enough as it is."

Eliza smiled. "Don't let us keep you, then. I'm suddenly rather hungry."

Eliza looked across to Archie as Miss Anderson headed towards a door on the opposite wall. "Why didn't you want me to tell her?"

"We can't go around alarming everyone. The police will do that this afternoon."

"I was hoping to speak to some of the staff about what they might have seen."

Archie rolled his eyes. "This investigation has nothing to do with us."

"It does if they think you and Father had anything to do with David's death. Did you see the change in the inspector when he found out you were the last ones to see him alive?" She paused when a waiter arrived with their lemonade. "Thank you. You can leave it there, I'll pour it."

"Not at all, madam. Allow me."

Eliza pursed her lips as he topped up each glass and rolled her eyes at Connie when he finally left. "Could he have taken any longer? Now, where was I?"

Archie tutted. "You weren't anywhere. We're leaving this investigation to the police. You've already done enough damage."

"I've done nothing of the sort. There's no harm in making a few enquiries ourselves." Eliza huffed and took a sip of lemonade. "Oh, that's nice."

"As I'm sure luncheon will be if you'll let us eat it in peace."

"I will, once you've told me exactly what happened last night. When we left you, there was a couple sitting on the table nearby. Did they stay in the bar as long as you?"

Archie looked at Mr Bell. "I think they did."

Mr Bell's forehead creased. "Didn't they leave about five minutes before us? It was them leaving that prompted us to go."

Archie nodded across several rows of tables. "They're over there, nearest the door. I didn't hear their names."

Mr Bell followed his gaze. "The couple on the table next

to them joined us shortly after you left and were still around as we went to bed. Colonel Giles, I think the waitress called him."

Eliza nodded. "He looks like the military sort. Was there anyone else nearby?"

"Not that I recall. Not within hearing distance, anyway."

Eliza leaned over to Connie. "We need to pick our seat carefully when we go into the lounge later."

Archie gritted his teeth. "Don't go telling everyone what's happened."

"I won't. I can be tactful. Now, what about David when he came back from the restaurant? How ill was he?"

"He was a little pale, but it wasn't obvious there was anything wrong. He said he'd had stomach cramps while he was out and so he ordered a large brandy."

"And you had one with him?"

"Not his first, but he said it had helped his stomach and insisted we have one with him when he had his second."

"Was he feeling better by the time you left?"

"I would say so. He didn't look as if he was at death's door."

"That's strange. The bathing machine definitely smelt as if he'd been ill."

Archie shrugged but said nothing as the waitress arrived with their plates.

"There you are. I'll bring some extra gravy in a minute."

Eliza licked her lips. "I'm not sure I'll manage all of this."

Mr Bell grinned. "We'll always help if you need us to."

They ate their meal in silence, but as she laid her knife and fork on her empty plate, Eliza studied Archie. "Did David tell you what he ate last night?"

"Steak and kidney pie."

"With mashed potato," Mr Bell added.

"So nothing that should have given him food poisoning."

"Not that he said."

"Which begs the question, why was he so ill? Didn't you notice the smell in the bathing machine?"

Archie shook his head. "I can't say I did. I was rather shocked at seeing him there."

She cocked her head to one side. "When you saw him, how was he lying? The outline under the sheet looked quite small."

"He was on his side with his knees pulled up towards his chest."

"As if he was in discomfort?"

"I suppose so."

"And what was he wearing? Was he still in his suit?"

Archie's forehead creased. "I think so."

"So he walked upstairs with you, but then shortly afterwards turned around and came down again."

"Why would it have been soon after?"

Eliza tutted. "Because if he'd had any plans to go to bed, he would have changed out of his suit."

"He could have dressed again. He wouldn't go outside in his pyjamas, however ill he felt."

"Maybe not, but if he was so ill that he needed to go to the sea, I doubt he'd bother putting his tie and jacket on. If it was me, I wouldn't get fully dressed again if I was ready for bed. Wouldn't you say he'd be more likely to come downstairs before he'd got undressed ... which would suggest it wasn't long after he got to his room." She sat back and stared at

Archie. "Can you think of anyone who would want him dead?"

"No, of course not."

Mr Bell dabbed his lips on a napkin. "You haven't seen him for a fair few years. You can't possibly know what's happened since you last met."

Archie huffed. "Whether I do or not, I know enough to recognise when Eliza's looking for trouble. The truth of the matter is that he probably ate too much and couldn't sleep, so decided to see if the water would help."

"Eating too much wouldn't make you that ill. I suggest we mention it to the doctor or police so that they examine the stomach contents during the post mortem."

"I'm sure Dr Poole is perfectly capable of doing the examination without your input. It's quite routine to check things like that."

"I don't doubt he'll check what David ate, but he won't think to test for poison unless he has reason to. From what I can see, the police haven't raised any grounds for suspicion."

"And would you like to tell him what to check for?"

Eliza ignored Archie's sarcasm. "I can't say for certain, but arsenic would be a good place to start. I'm sure he's aware of other tests if that proves negative."

"And when he finds nothing, will you stop interfering with the investigation?"

"*If* he finds nothing, then yes, I will, but I've a feeling you'll find I'm right."

## CHAPTER FIVE

Eliza placed her china cup on its saucer and returned it to the occasional table in front of her. The lounge was busy after luncheon, and she watched the staff scurry from table to table with orders.

"They never seem to stop."

Mr Bell peered over the top of his newspaper. "They do work in the most exclusive hotel in the country. It's no wonder."

"I know, but still..." She paused as Inspector Jarvis appeared in the archway adjoining the foyer. "He's here."

"Who?" Archie turned in his chair. "Ah, he's seen us." He stood up as the inspector approached and shook his hand. "Will you join us? I can ask the waitress for another cup and saucer."

"I will, if you don't mind. I've been on my feet all morning."

Archie beckoned Miss Anderson over and requested a selection of cakes and hot water along with the crockery.

Once she'd gone, he turned back to the inspector. "Do you have any news for us?"

Inspector Jarvis hesitated as he glanced at Eliza and Connie, but Archie waved a dismissive arm at them.

"As I mentioned earlier, you can speak in front of my wife and her companion. I'll only have to repeat all the details once you've gone, if you don't."

The inspector sighed. "Very well. We've had the preliminary findings back from Dr Poole and he's confirmed that the cause of death was drowning. It looks like the gentleman was in the bathing machine when the tide came in and it caught him unawares. I suspect we'll find it was a tragic accident."

"Very tragic." Archie nodded but said no more as Eliza bit her tongue. When he remained silent, she interrupted. "Has Dr Poole examined the contents of Dr Shaw's stomach yet?"

The inspector gave her a piercing look. "I presume he has, but I doubt it would be a priority given the victim drowned."

"I understand that, but I feel the question needs to be asked as to why he drowned. You're suggesting it may have been an accident, but I'm afraid that doesn't fit with what we know of Dr Shaw. He wouldn't make such a silly mistake without reason."

"Well, no one bundled him into the bathing machine, if that's what you mean. There were no signs of a struggle."

"No, that's not what I mean." Eliza took a deep breath. "I've been wondering if it had anything to do with Dr Shaw's upset stomach. He was as right as rain when we saw him leave the hotel to go to a restaurant, but he wasn't feeling well when he came back. The smell in the bathing machine confirms someone had been ill in there, presumably before the sea washed all the evidence away."

"So you're suggesting he ate some dubious seafood?"

"Not at all. According to my husband, he dined on steak and kidney pie with mashed potato. Hardly the sort of food to make you ill."

"So, what are you getting at?"

Archie raised a hand. "Forgive my wife, Inspector. She's been involved in several investigations into suspicious deaths over the last few years, and what she's trying to say is that there's a possibility that Dr Shaw may have been poisoned."

"Poisoned! I've just told you, he drowned."

"Yes, but there's a chance the stomach ache is important ... it may be why he was less attentive to the tide than he should have been." Archie grimaced. "It's a long shot, obviously ... but could you mention it to Dr Poole?"

Eliza leaned across the table. "I'd suggest he start with arsenic..."

Archie pulled her back. "That's enough. The inspector and Dr Poole will know what to do."

Inspector Jarvis stood up. "Quite. Now, if you'll excuse me."

"Won't you stay for tea?" Connie pointed across the room. "The waitress is here now."

Miss Anderson's face coloured as she joined them. "I'm sorry to take so long. I've been rushed off my feet."

"There's no need to apologise." Eliza glared at their guest. "The inspector's just realised he needs to pay someone a visit."

"Inspector?" She placed the tray on the table and stood up. "Is this about the incident this morning?"

Inspector Jarvis stared at her. "What about it?"

"Nothing ... b-but I saw policemen going to the beach."

"Well, let's leave it that way, shall we? We don't want you worrying your little head about it."

"Oh." Miss Anderson looked down at the cakes as he walked away and then back to Eliza. "Will you still be wanting these?"

She checked the clock. "You can leave them, thank you. We've wasted so much time waiting for the inspector to turn up, it's almost time for afternoon tea. If you could just freshen up the teapot..."

"Very well." Miss Anderson hunched her shoulders as she wandered to the next table.

"That wasn't very nice of the inspector, speaking to her like that."

Archie gasped. "Are you surprised after you upset him?"

"Why did I upset him? I was only offering a suggestion. It's not my fault he was offended."

"It's always the same, as well you know. Inspectors aren't all like Inspector Adams."

Connie chuckled by her side. "Even he didn't want our help when we first met him."

Eliza straightened her back and reached for a cake. "He wouldn't have solved that murder if it hadn't been for us. I just need to show this inspector how helpful we can be."

"You'll do nothing of the sort. Just leave it." Archie's cheeks coloured. "Hopefully, he'll ask Dr Poole to check for poisoning, but if he doesn't, there's not much we can do about it."

"We could inform the coroner."

"And upset him further?"

Eliza huffed. "David was our friend, in case you'd forgotten. Don't you want to find out what happened to him?"

"Of course I do, but I'd like to hear it from the police. Now, can we talk about something else?"

"I can do better than that. Once we've finished this tea, I'd like to take a walk ... with Connie." She turned to her friend. "Will you join me, so we can leave these two to their peace and quiet?"

"I'd like that. It feels as if we've been sitting around for hours."

"Splendid. Let's hurry up here so we can get out of their way."


Eliza couldn't get out of the lounge quickly enough, but Connie raised an eyebrow when they reached the foyer and Eliza's pace slowed.

"What's the matter? I thought you wanted to go outside."

"I do. And we will ... in a minute." She studied the door and porters' desk. "I want a word with the doorman. He may have some information for us."

Connie chased after her. "Like what?"

She raised an eyebrow. "Let's go and find out."

A tall, middle-aged man dressed in an elegant black morning suit held open the door as they approached, but Eliza stopped and glanced at his name badge. "Thank you, Mr Topham. It's another lovely day."

"It is indeed, madam. Are the gentlemen not joining you this afternoon?"

Eliza grinned. "They wanted to read their newspapers, so

we've left them to it." She peered through the door to the other side of the road. "I saw several policemen outside earlier. Do you know whether they're still there?"

"I believe they've gone, but I can't see the beach from here, so there may be one or two still around. Several officers came into the hotel to speak to some of us earlier, but they left around an hour ago."

She studied him. "So you're aware of what all the fuss was about?"

"I can't say I am. They didn't give much away."

"Are you able to tell us what they asked?"

"I'm afraid not. They spoke to me and several of the porters who were working yesterday evening, but they asked us to keep the conversations to ourselves."

"Oh, I see. I can understand why they'd want to speak to you, though. It must be a very responsible job keeping your eye on everyone coming and going. I'm surprised you're here now if you were here until late last night."

"It's not a problem. When I work until midnight, I don't start until three o'clock in the afternoon."

"Gracious. Do you do that every day?"

"Every other week. The alternate weeks I work from six in the morning until three in the afternoon. The night porters take over from midnight until six in the morning. Not that I always leave bang on twelve. It was about a quarter past when I left last night with all the commotion."

Eliza cocked her head to one side. "That sounds intriguing."

"Oh, it was something and nothing in the end. Not anything for you to worry about."

"Well, I don't know how you do it, especially not so late."

He straightened his back and puffed out his chest. "There's always something to occupy me."

"I'm glad to hear it." She looked at Connie. "Are you ready to go?"

Connie rolled her eyes. "I'm waiting for you."

"Oh, yes. Let's go, then. Thank you, Mr Topham." Eliza skipped down the hotel steps as Connie followed her.

"What was all that about?"

"I wanted to check who was on the door last night when David went outside ... and now we know. We could do with finding out which porters were working, too, but they were all busy. Now we're on speaking terms with Mr Topham, we can ask him."

They crossed the road, and Eliza headed to the steps leading down to the beach. She offered Connie the chance to go first, but her friend paused.

"Why are we going down there again? It was hard enough to walk on the pebbles when I was holding your father's arm."

"It's not far, and look, they've pulled the bathing machines up the beach already."

Connie studied the cabins lined up along the sea wall. "What a shame they weren't all there last night. Dr Shaw wouldn't have drowned if they had been."

Eliza put a hand on Connie's arm. "Of course!" She hurried down the steps and surveyed the beach. "Most of the machines were here this morning. I assumed the dippers had found David's body after they had moved the one he was in, but what if someone had already moved it?"

"What do you mean?"

"If someone deliberately wanted David dead, they may have moved the machine last night..."

"Don't you think the tide could have carried it?"

Eliza studied the sand between the pebbles. "I doubt it. The pebbles here are dry, suggesting the sea doesn't come this far up the beach."

"So, you think someone deliberately moved it?"

"It's a possibility." She shook her head. "Whoever moved it must have known where to leave it so the water would come high enough up to cover the floor."

"They'd have to be strong. Unless there was more than one of them." Connie tried to lift one of the arms extending from the front of a machine. "I couldn't move it."

Eliza lifted the arm on the other side. "It is heavy."

"Do you think Dr Shaw could have moved it himself? He had planned to go into the water..."

"I doubt he'd have had the strength if he had an upset stomach." Eliza wandered around the line of bathing machines. "I'll ask Archie to lift it when we're next here. See how difficult it is for him."

Connie studied her. "Are you sure? He won't be happy if he knows we've been investigating."

"You're probably right."

They continued to stare at the machine until Connie stood between the two arms protruding from the front.

"Maybe Dr Shaw's friend helped him move it."

"Perhaps, but whoever he was with should have known how far up the beach the tide would come."

"Unless they're not from Brighton."

"Or they wanted him dead." Eliza bit on her bottom lip.

"We need to find out more about the man David had dinner with."

"You think it could be him?"

"It has to be a consideration." She glanced around the beach. "We need to find out when the machine was moved, too."

"Are you thinking the drowning might not have been accidental?"

"I'd say there's a distinct possibility. We need to determine whether David was in the bathing machine at the time someone moved it, or whether it was down the beach before he climbed in?"

"How do we prove it either way?"

"That's a good question. If the police think he died between midnight and three o'clock, we need to find someone who was able to see the beach at midnight, and hope they noticed the position of the machines."

"Is that likely?"

Eliza shrugged. "Probably not, especially given how dark it would have been, but we could ask the doorman if he saw anything."

"He said he can't see the beach from where he stands."

"He may have had cause to walk across the road if the commotion he mentioned happened outside the hotel. I would have done."

Connie laughed. "I don't doubt it. If it really was a commotion, some guests may have seen something."

Eliza rested her chin on her right index finger. "You'd think so, the number of people in the hotel. We'll need to ask around. It's a shame the dippers are finished for the day. We need to talk to the person who found the body."

"Shouldn't we wait before we speak to anyone else? We haven't had confirmation it was murder yet?"

"We may not know whether he was poisoned, but he died in a bathing machine that was inexplicably partway down the beach. I'd say that's a good enough reason to suggest his death was anything but accidental."

# CHAPTER SIX

A rchie and Mr Bell were nowhere to be seen when they returned to the lounge, but Eliza walked past their usual seat by the window and found a table closer to the guests at the far end of the room. She whispered to Connie as she sat down.

"We may be able to eavesdrop on a few conversations from here. It's less secluded."

Connie chuckled. "I thought there'd be a reason for moving."

Eliza smiled at the two elderly ladies sitting at the next table. "Good afternoon. It's been a lovely day."

"Oh, it has." The woman who sat the taller of the two nodded to her companion. "We walked up to our friend's house just along the coast, and we were rather warm by the time we got there."

"That's nice that you know someone in the area."

"Oh, she's the reason we come to Brighton. We live just outside London, and she did, too, until one day she announced she was upping sticks and coming here to be near the sea. Just like that. It ruined our bridge parties."

The smaller of the women adjusted the pince-nez that perched on the end of her nose. "I think she felt guilty once she'd left, which is why she invites us here at the beginning of every month."

"How lovely to be able to visit so often."

"It is at this time of the year, but it's quite another matter in winter. We've told her she must start coming to us instead."

Eliza grinned. "You'll have to tempt her with the shopping in London." She sat back as the waitress joined them.

"Good afternoon, ladies. Are you on your own today?"

"Good afternoon, Mrs Dunn. Yes, we are. It's nice to see you again. I was beginning to think you were avoiding us."

"Me? No. W-why would I?" Her eyes flicked between Eliza and Connie.

"No reason, I'm only teasing. Miss Anderson told us you sometimes swap tables."

"Were you looking for me?"

"No, not at all. We just thought we'd like a change of scenery ourselves."

"Ah, right. What may I get you?"

"Do you have any of the lemonade we had yesterday? It was rather nice."

"We certainly do. Will that be two?"

"Please." Connie smiled as the waitress left and Eliza turned back to the ladies beside them.

"Forgive us for not introducing ourselves. I'm Mrs Thomson, and this is my companion, Mrs Appleton."

The taller woman straightened the rim of her feather-covered hat. "Pleased to make your acquaintance. I'm Mrs Smith and this is my sister-in-law, Mrs Gardener."

"Do your husbands travel with you?"

Mrs Gardener sighed. "We're both widowed, I'm afraid."

"Ah. I'm sorry to hear that."

Mrs Smith tutted. "Don't worry about us. We're quite used to it now, and it means we're able to suit ourselves. They left us well provided for..."

"That's fortunate." Eliza lowered her voice. "Were you around to see the police on the beach this morning?"

"Police? No!" Mrs Smith stared at her companion. "What did we miss?"

Eliza bit her lip. "They've been quite secretive. That's why I asked..."

"Oh, what a shame. We like something to talk about, but we've been at our friend's house for most of the day. You will tell us if you hear anything?"

"Yes, of course, but–" Eliza leaned across to them as Archie and Mr Bell appeared, "–we'll wait until we're on our own." She smiled at Archie as he and Mr Bell approached. "Here you are. We've just introduced ourselves to Mrs Smith and Mrs Gardener. Ladies, this is my husband, Dr Thomson, and my father, Mr Bell."

After a round of greetings, the men took their seats, and Archie studied their surroundings. "Don't you like our usual seat?"

"I thought we'd see what's going on up here for a change."

Mr Bell adjusted his jacket. "Have you ordered?"

"We have. Two glasses of lemonade. Mrs Dunn won't be long. In fact, she's here now."

"Oh." Mrs Dunn glared down at them. "You said you were on your own."

"I'm sorry. We weren't expecting company when we arrived."

"And what about the other gentleman you were with last night? Will he be joining you?"

Eliza's mouth fell open, and she looked at Archie for an answer.

"No. Not today."

Mrs Dunn pursed her lips. "Good. Right. May I get you anything?"

Mr Bell pointed to the drinks she placed on the table. "The lemonade looks nice. Two of them?" He raised an eyebrow at Archie, who nodded.

"Please. And I promise we're not expecting anyone else."

Eliza's forehead creased as Mrs Dunn left them. "How strange. She doesn't seem to like it when people join us unexpectedly."

Connie shrugged. "It probably makes more work for her. If we'd all been here together, she'd have finished our order by now, but as it is..."

"You're right. It's still rather odd behaviour, though."

Mr Bell studied Eliza and Connie as they took a sip of their drinks. "What have you been up to since we last saw you?"

"Not much. We've been back to the beach to see if we missed anything earlier."

"You've been down there again?"

"It was a worthwhile visit." She lowered her voice as she huddled towards them. "Did you notice the position of the bathing machine when they found David's body? It was halfway down the beach."

Archie rolled his eyes. "That's where they usually are. People who want to hide their modesty can't go into the sea when the machine's near the wall."

"I know that, but they found David at about ten o'clock this morning, when the dippers arrived. The cabin should still have been at the top of the beach with the others."

"They may have moved it before they opened the door."

"Hmm." Eliza glanced at Connie and then back to Archie. "I'm sure they'd have noticed the extra weight."

"Perhaps..."

"And they hadn't moved any of the others." Connie's voice was soft, but Eliza almost jumped from her chair.

"Exactly! Why would they move that one but none of the others?"

Archie tutted. "It was on the end, nearest the steps. It would be the first one they came to."

"We still need to check if they were the ones who moved it. They'd left the beach before we realised we needed to speak to them."

"Who else would move it? The chances are, the dippers arrived, moved the first machine in the row, then opened it up to find David inside."

"Not if someone wanted David dead. They would have wanted it further down the beach so the water would cover him."

"That's highly unlikely, but if it was, I'm sure the police will find out."

"Really? I'm not. They still seem to be treating this as a freak accident, and I don't like it."

Archie held up his hands. "All right, if it keeps you quiet, I'll take another look at it tomorrow."

"And will you mention it to Inspector Jarvis?"

He sighed. "If I must."

# CHAPTER SEVEN

A thin layer of cloud covered the sky when they arrived in the dining room the following morning, and Eliza gazed out of the window as they waited for the waitress.

"At least we can see properly this morning, with no sun and the curtains open. Not that there's much to see."

Connie followed her gaze. "It's a marvellous view."

"It is, but other than a procession of people walking one way or the other, there's nothing going on. I wonder if the dippers have arrived yet."

Mr Bell checked his pocket watch. "I doubt it. It's only half past eight. It was ten o'clock before they found the body yesterday."

"That may be because it was Sunday. I expect they'll be here earlier today." Eliza placed a napkin on her lap. "I hope Dr Poole doesn't take too long with the post mortem. I presume he'll examine the stomach contents more thoroughly this morning."

Archie shrugged. "Only if he has nothing else urgent. And assuming Inspector Jarvis passed on the message."

"I'll be mad if he didn't." Eliza pursed her lips as the waitress arrived.

"Good morning." Miss Anderson smiled as she stood with her pencil poised over her paper. "Did you all sleep well?"

"Yes, thank you." Eliza turned to her. "You may know the answer to this. What time do the dippers start work during the week?"

"Oh, early. They'll probably be here already. There are many gents who like to go in the sea before breakfast."

"I hadn't thought of that." She grimaced at Archie and Mr Bell. "We'd better not spend too long on breakfast."

"I'm sure there's no rush." Archie looked up at Miss Anderson. "What time do they finish of an evening?"

"Not until about five o'clock, so you've plenty of time if you'd like to go into the sea yourself."

"Oh, it's not that..." Eliza stopped as Archie glared at her. "We ... erm ... we were just wondering how long they worked."

"Then the answer is from early morning until five o'clock, although the donkey rides don't start until ten."

"Donkey rides! Gracious, I won't be going on one of them."

Miss Anderson laughed. "Maybe not, but it's still lovely to see the kiddies on them. Now, what may I get you for breakfast?"

After ordering and eating the same breakfast as the day before, they all ventured down to the beach. The dippers were on the edge of the sea, helping a group of hapless women into the water and dunking their heads under the waves. Eliza shuddered.

"There's not a chance you'll get me to do that."

Archie shook his head. "Look how pleased they are when they come out. Wouldn't you like to feel invigorated like that?"

"No, I wouldn't." She stepped closer to the bathing machine nearest to them and waited until the last of the group had retreated inside before she approached the dipper. "Excuse me. Do you mind if I ask you a question?"

A large woman with her navy dress tucked into her undergarments walked towards them. "There's a queue."

"Oh, I don't wish to go in. I just wondered who found the body in the machine yesterday."

"That'll be Mabel." She pointed to a similarly dressed woman at the next machine. "Gave her quite a fright, it did."

"I don't doubt it. Thank you."

Mabel appeared to be thoroughly enjoying herself dipping an unsuspecting young girl under the waves, and Archie and Mr Bell averted their eyes as the entertainment ended and the girl scrambled up the steps into the cabin. Eliza and Connie walked to the water's edge as the woman tucked several stray pieces of hair back under her hat.

"Mabel?"

"That's me."

"I'm sorry to interrupt, but I believe you found the body yesterday."

"I most certainly did." She put a hand to her chest. "I've never been so shocked in my life. Just lying there he was. Anyway, what of it?"

Eliza cleared her throat. "Unfortunately, the man you found was a friend of ours, and I'm interested in finding out what happened. I heard that the bathing machine had been moved from the back wall..."

"It had ... but not by me. I was the first here and hurried straight to it when I saw where it was."

"And at that stage, had the tide gone out far enough to see the body?"

"It most certainly had. It left a right smell, too."

"Yes, I noticed that. May I ask if there's any chance it could have rolled down the beach by itself?"

She shook her head. "None. They were all tied up on Saturday night when I left, so someone had deliberately moved it. Goodness knows when, though. It gets very dark down here at night."

Connie cocked her head to one side. "We didn't leave the hotel on Saturday night, but the moon must have been near the full."

The dipper nodded. "That would help, but I couldn't tell you how much cloud cover there was. Now, if you don't mind, I need to get this machine up the beach."

Eliza and Connie stepped back and joined Archie and Mr Bell as another dipper led a horse towards them and hitched it to the machine.

"So that's how they do it." Eliza watched with fascination as Connie stood beside her.

"They couldn't have done that at midnight."

"No." Eliza let out a deep sigh as Archie took her arm.

"Come on, let's take a walk instead of brooding over this. It will become clear soon enough."


The foyer was busy when they returned from their walk, and Archie ushered them to the archway on the right-hand side of the door.

"I presume we're going straight to the dining room."

"Ah." Eliza looked at Connie. "I had hoped to freshen up and change these shoes. My feet are rather warm."

Connie laughed. "I'm glad it's not just me. We can be quick."

"Yes, let's do that." She turned to Archie. "Why don't you and Father go and sit at the table and we'll join you in five minutes?"

Archie raised his eyebrows. "I'll have to hope Mrs Dunn isn't serving today. She won't be pleased if you're late."

"She'll be fine if you tell her we're coming, and you could order a couple of lemonades for us while you wait."

Connie smiled. "That would be nice."

"Very well, but don't be long. It feels like an age since breakfast."

Connie glanced at the grand staircase as Eliza put a foot on the first step. "Aren't we taking the lift?"

Eliza pointed into the corner of the foyer. "Have you seen the number of people waiting to go up? We'll be quicker walking."

"If you say so." Connie sighed as they started their ascent, but as they reached the first landing and turned to go up the next half flight of stairs, Eliza's face broke into a grin.

"Poor Archie. Did you see his reaction when we told him the dippers had found the bathing machine where we saw it yesterday morning? He was adamant he was right about them moving it with David inside."

Connie chuckled. "It was rather funny. It's as well Mr Bell was with us, or he may have asked all the other dippers, to be sure."

"He really should trust my instincts by now. I knew they

wouldn't have moved it. At least it means we can return to our original line of thinking. Was David in the cabin before it was moved or didn't he arrive until later?"

They were out of breath when they arrived on the second floor and they walked to Connie's room in silence. Eliza waited while Connie found her key.

"Give me five minutes and I'll meet you back here."


Connie was waiting outside her room when Eliza returned wearing a fresh cream blouse and a new pair of summer shoes.

"You didn't say you were getting changed, as well."

Eliza gave an apologetic smile. "I couldn't help myself after being down there."

"Should I change, too?"

"You'd better not. Father will be getting impatient. Besides, you're fine as you are."

"As long as you're sure."

"Of course I am." Eliza led the way into the dining room, but stopped halfway across the foyer and held out an arm to keep Connie where she was. "The inspector's here."

"Where?"

"At our table."

"Do you think he's got the results of the post mortem?"

"There's only one way to find out." Eliza straightened her skirt, and then her shoulders, as she strode purposefully towards the table. "Inspector Jarvis. Are you joining us?"

"No, not at all." He stood up and acknowledged Connie before he turned back to Archie. "I suggest we meet in the lounge at two o'clock."

Archie nodded. "I'll be there."

Eliza took her seat as the inspector left. "He was rather abrupt. What was that about?"

"He's had the results of the post mortem."

"And..."

Archie's face twisted as he held her gaze. "You were right..."

Eliza grinned at him. "I knew it! Was it arsenic?"

"It was. The cause of death was still recorded as drowning, but David had enough arsenic in his stomach to kill him ... if he'd lived long enough. He was probably unconscious when the tide came in, which would be why it didn't wake him."

"Gracious. That explains a lot."

Connie's forehead creased. "How did someone give him such a large amount?"

Archie linked his fingers together and rested his index fingers on his chin. "That's a good question. The most likely explanation is that someone added it to his drinks. It would take more than one dose for him not to notice."

Eliza nodded. "At least two, I would say. Why does the inspector want to speak to you at two o'clock? Does he want your help in the investigation?"

"Not in the way you think." Archie huffed. "He asked how we knew they'd find arsenic in the stomach."

"Because I've been paying attention to the details, and it seemed likely..."

"I know that, and I tried to tell him, but along with your father, I was one of the last people to see David alive, and the inspector has a vivid imagination."

"What?" Eliza's eyes darted between the two of them. "He can't think one of you poisoned him. If you had, why would we say anything about it? It would have passed unnoticed if we'd kept quiet."

"He didn't think that was much of an excuse."

"Does he want to talk to all of us?"

"Only me and then your father this afternoon, but he'll want to see you and Mrs Appleton at some point, given you were with us before David went for dinner ... and because you were the one who suggested we test for arsenic."

"I did it to help, not get you into trouble."

"I know..."

Miss Anderson appeared by Eliza's side and placed four glasses of lemonade on the table. "I'm sorry I'm late with these. There's a police officer in the hotel and he chose now of all times to speak to me. As if I've not got enough to do."

"He spoke to you? What did he want to know?"

Miss Anderson looked around. "I can't talk at the moment. I'm behind as it is. I'll tell you later if you're around. Have you decided what you'd like to eat?"

Eliza grimaced. "No, I'm sorry. We've been busy talking. You serve your other guests and come back. We're in no hurry."

"I will, thank you."

Archie waited until Miss Anderson was out of earshot. "You may not be in a hurry, but I have less than an hour before my meeting with the inspector."

"Well, he can wait if he's daft enough to think you had anything to do with David's death."

"That will make it worse..."

"Nonsense. He has no evidence against you ... and we'll prove it."

# CHAPTER EIGHT

A t two minutes to two, Eliza walked into the lounge on Archie's arm and stayed with him as he approached Inspector Jarvis. He stood up as Archie offered him a hand.

"Dr Thomson. Mrs Thomson." He smirked at Eliza. "I think you misunderstood. It's your husband I wish to speak to."

Eliza fixed her smile. "I understood that perfectly well, but if you have any notion that he, or anyone else in our party, was responsible for Dr Shaw's death, then I need to be here, as well."

"We'll get to you later, Mrs Thomson. At the moment, I'm just following a line of enquiry, nothing more."

"Why don't we save you some time, then?"

The inspector gasped at Archie as Eliza took a seat. "This is most unusual."

Archie's cheek creased. "You'll get used to it."

"Very well." The inspector hesitated as he flicked back through his notebook. "Right. Dr Thomson, you told me yesterday that you had spent the evening with Dr Shaw and had walked up the stairs with him at around half past eleven. Can you confirm that?"

"I can. I've already told you I was with my father-in-law, Mr Bell, and we can vouch for each other."

"But no one else can. Not Mrs Thomson, if I understand correctly."

"No, my wife was asleep when I got back to the room."

"And what about Mr Bell? I believe he would have been on his own. Did he leave you while you were still with Dr Shaw?"

"Erm ... yes, he did. We stopped in the corridor as he let himself in and then we carried on to my room before Dr Shaw walked to his."

"So there was a minute or more when you and the deceased were alone?" The inspector raised an eyebrow. "Was there anyone else in the corridor to confirm your movements?"

Archie stared at the inspector. "Not that I'm aware of, but I wasn't paying attention."

Eliza gasped. "This is nonsense..."

The inspector turned his gaze on her. "If you must sit there, Mrs Thomson, I'd appreciate it if you didn't interrupt. There's a good thing. Now..." he returned to his notes "...who arranged the meeting in the lounge?"

"Well ... we both did. Dr Shaw and I, but it was only an informal arrangement. We'd seen him when he was leaving the hotel and he said he'd look out for us when he got back."

"He didn't eat in the hotel?"

"No. He was meeting an old acquaintance at a restaurant in town, but I'm afraid I don't know which one."

The inspector sneered at Eliza. "Did he, by any chance, mention it to you...?"

"No, he didn't, but I imagine one of the porters or the doorman will know, especially if they arranged a carriage for him."

"I'm aware of that, but I was hoping you could save me some time."

Eliza's eyes narrowed, but she said nothing, causing him to scribble something in his notebook.

"Right. We'll follow up on that. Dr Thomson, you said Dr Shaw was feeling unwell when he joined you?"

"Yes, he had a stomach ache. He thought at the time he must have eaten too much, but with hindsight, I would say it was because he'd already ingested some poison."

"The time of death has been recorded as somewhere between midnight and three o'clock, but you're trying to tell me he'd been poisoned before then."

"Yes, that's right."

"Just like that. Someone poisoned him with arsenic, but he still managed to stroll into the hotel for a drink?"

"It's not as improbable as it sounds."

"We'll leave that for Dr Poole to decide..."

Eliza leaned forward in her chair. "Forgive me, Inspector, but do you know much about arsenic poisoning?"

"I'm fully aware that it's one of the most commonly used agents for those up to no good and has led to the deaths of far too many people."

"But you don't seem to understand how it works. Perhaps you should ask Dr Poole about it."

His left eye twitched. "Why don't you save me the trouble and tell me yourself?"

"I'm sure you don't need full chapter and verse, but you seem to have missed the point that it can take hours, if not days, for a seemingly lethal dose of arsenic to kill a person. This isn't cyanide we're talking about..."

"And how is it you know so much about it? It's often said that poison is a woman's method of choice should she wish to be rid of someone..."

"Then let me put you straight." Eliza took a deep breath. "When we're at home, I work as my husband's pharmacy dispenser. I need to be familiar with things like this."

The inspector's eyes shifted from Eliza to Archie and back again. "So you're both involved? Did you plan to provide the poison while your husband slipped it into Dr Shaw's drink when he wasn't looking? Is that why you wanted to speak to me together...?"

Eliza groaned. "Why would we do that? We didn't even know Dr Shaw was staying here until we bumped into him."

"That doesn't rule out the fact you could have bought some rat poison when you arrived in Brighton."

Eliza huffed. "I've never heard such nonsense, but if you're prepared to waste your time checking all the local grocery stores and chemists, specifically looking for the variety with no added dye, then be my guest."

"I'm sure my constable would be delighted to. Now, where were we?" He returned to his notes. "You said Dr Shaw returned to the hotel after he'd taken dinner in a restaurant and found you in the lounge?"

"He did, and there were other guests sitting nearby who could confirm that."

The inspector held his pencil over his notepad. "Their names, please, sir."

Archie looked exasperated. "I've no idea. We didn't introduce ourselves."

"That's convenient."

"I'd recognise them again if I saw them. I've since seen two of the couples in the dining room, so they won't be hard to find." Archie pulled a clean handkerchief from his pocket and wiped his brow.

"Excellent. I'll join you later to see if you can spot them..."

Eliza scowled across the table. "I fail to see what you're hoping to achieve with this line of questioning. Dr Shaw was a friend to both of us, although we hadn't seen him for years. Why would we want him dead?"

He sneered at her. "A very good question, and one I hope you can answer. How well were you acquainted with Dr Shaw? Before this weekend."

"Me? W-we spent time together many years ago when he was at medical school and I was at Bedford College. It's part of London University in case you're wondering. Our faculties would often socialise together."

"You were at university?" The inspector's mouth fell open.

"Is there something wrong?"

"The plot thickens. An apparently educated woman studying with all those men. Was he an old flame who was pleased to see you again?"

"Not at all." Eliza shot Archie a look. "He was the one who introduced me to Dr Thomson, if you must know, and he came to our wedding with a young lady we expected him to marry."

"But he didn't? Would that be because he still carried a

torch for you? And your husband was jealous when he saw the two of you together again…?"

Archie banged a hand on the table. "Inspector Jarvis. May I remind you that this is my wife you're talking to? She and Dr Shaw were no more than acquaintances, and I won't have you suggesting anything else. Neither of us has any motive for wanting our friend dead, but even if we were the ones to poison his drinks, why would we ask you to check for it as part of the post mortem? Until we raised it, you and Dr Poole would have settled for accidental death by drowning and we wouldn't be having this conversation now."

The inspector's cheeks flushed. "I'm only confirming the facts, sir, and with all due respect, by your own admission, you weren't with your wife at any time after half past nine. Perhaps only one of you is our killer, and it was the other who suggested he may have been poisoned, without realising the trouble they were causing."

"What nonsense…"

"Is it really?" The inspector's eyes narrowed as he held Eliza's gaze. "Was it you who asked Dr Shaw to meet you outside at midnight?"

"Me? No, how could I? I didn't see him once he'd gone to dinner."

"You were on your own for two hours after you'd gone upstairs. That's plenty of time to write a note and push it underneath his door."

Eliza's eyes widened as she stared at Archie. "What note? That's the first we've heard of it."

Inspector Jarvis produced a sheet of paper from his inside pocket and held it between Archie and Eliza.

"It's clearly written in a woman's handwriting, which may

explain why Dr Shaw didn't need any persuading to go back downstairs ... and you're very familiar with poisons."

Eliza's heart pounded as she read the note. *We need to talk. Meet me outside at midnight.* She gaped at the inspector. "I had no need to speak to him privately. As I explained earlier, if I was going to poison him at such short notice, I wouldn't have chosen arsenic. That's not even my handwriting..."

"We'll be checking that shortly, madam, but until we've made an arrest, I'd be obliged if you remain in Brighton."

Archie jumped to his feet. "Listen here, Inspector. I realise you need to find the killer, but there is no need to make insinuations about my wife's character that are nothing more than slanderous lies. The truth of the matter appears to be that someone poisoned Dr Shaw, then, to make it appear as if it was an accident, they enticed him out of the hotel and put him in a bathing machine so the sea would do the rest. Neither my wife nor I had the motive or opportunity to do either of those things, so I suggest you start speaking to someone who did."

# CHAPTER NINE

E liza's hands were still shaking when Connie strolled down the promenade beside Archie and joined her on a bench overlooking the sea.

Archie placed a hand on his wife's shoulder. "I'll leave the two of you together. Join us for afternoon tea when you're ready."

"We will, thank you."

Connie watched him leave. "Are you all right? Dr Thomson said Inspector Jarvis had upset you."

"He's a fool of a man. Did Archie tell you he was intent on ruining my reputation so he could set me up as the murderer?"

"No!" Connie's eyes widened as Eliza nodded.

"He decided I must have been *close* to David when we were younger and that he still held a torch for me..."

"You weren't, were you?"

Eliza gasped. "Of course I wasn't."

"Don't look at me like that. I was only checking. If it's not true, why would he even think of it?"

"Because he's an idiot. At first, he inferred that Archie had become jealous when he'd seen me with David, and had wanted him out of the way, but then he turned the blame on me."

"Why?"

"Someone wrote a letter asking David to meet them outside at midnight and pushed it under his door. The inspector jumped to the conclusion that it was me who wanted to see him, and that I'd have had plenty of time to write a note and deliver it once we'd gone upstairs. He even made me copy out the message to check my handwriting. Thankfully, it was nothing like the script on the original."

Connie shuddered. "I hope he doesn't suspect me of writing it for you."

"We'll find out soon enough, if he does."

"What do you mean?"

"Only that he'll want to see your handwriting, too. It wouldn't surprise me if he's waiting for us when we get back to the hotel."

Connie's face paled. "Oh gracious."

"Don't worry. I saw the original letter, and the script is nothing like yours."

"You're sure?"

"Positive. If you write as you normally do, you'll be fine."

Connie bit down on her lip. "I hope so. It all seems so unnecessary. Even if one of us had written it, you wouldn't have been able to go outside that late at night. Dr Thomson was back in the room by then…"

"I know."

"…but I would…" Connie's eyes widened. "I have no one to confirm where I was."

Eliza tutted. "What possible motive would you have for poisoning David? You didn't meet him until Saturday."

"But you did. What if Inspector Jarvis thinks I did it because you asked me to...?"

"And why would I do that when I was the one who suggested checking for arsenic?"

"He may think you were trying to get me into trouble..."

"Which goes to show he has no idea what he's doing."

"But that won't save me from jail..." Connie's voice was a pitch too high, and Eliza took her hand.

"Come on, calm down. You're not going anywhere near jail. Sergeant Cooper will be here tomorrow, and he'll vouch for you. Archie was pretty angry with the inspector too, so he won't let anything happen."

"I hope you're right."

"Of course I am."

Connie took a deep breath. "We just need to find out who really did it."

"Oh, don't you worry. We will. There's not a chance I'm going to sit back and leave this investigation to Inspector Jarvis. The chances of him finding the right killer are zero, and I'll make sure he realises how incompetent he is before we've finished."

Archie and Mr Bell stood up and pulled out two chairs for them when they arrived in the lounge.

Archie ran a finger down Eliza's cheek as she settled herself. "Have you calmed down?"

"I'm not shaking any more, if that's what you mean. I'm glad you were with me. Heaven knows what I'd have said if

I'd been on my own." She looked at her father. "I presume Archie told you what happened."

"He did, and I gave the inspector a piece of my mind when I saw him. He shouldn't trouble you any more."

"He'd better not harass Connie, either."

Connie's cheeks flushed as Archie turned to her. "Why would he do that?"

"He may think I wrote the letter for Eliza ... so it wasn't obvious she was the one who wanted to meet Dr Shaw."

"Nonsense."

Eliza gave Archie a faint smile. "She's worried she has no alibi."

"If you want my opinion, the fact the letter doesn't match her handwriting should be enough, but if it isn't, nobody can say they saw her in the foyer after about half past nine."

Connie's shoulders relaxed. "You're right, thank you. I was being silly."

Eliza glanced around the room. "Is the inspector still in the hotel?"

Archie nodded. "It looks like he's taken my advice and started talking to some of the staff and guests. Your father reminded me of the names of one couple who were in the lounge when David joined us. Colonel and Mrs Giles. My mind went blank when the inspector asked."

"I remember them now. You pointed them out at luncheon."

Archie shook his head. "He had me in such a flap."

"Well, the inspector isn't the only one who can speak to them. I'll see if I can catch them later, and anyone else I can find. First, I suggest we start with the barman and waitresses.

They clearly had the opportunity to slip something into David's drink, but did they have a motive?"

Archie patted her hand. "After what happened earlier, if you need my help, just ask."

Miss Anderson distracted them when she arrived at the table. "Good afternoon, ladies. Gentlemen. I hope I'm not disturbing anything. You look deep in conversation."

Eliza smiled. "Nothing that can't wait. We'd like afternoon tea for four, please, but I wonder if you have a moment to talk before you go."

She glanced around the rest of her tables. "I've probably got a couple of minutes. Everyone seems settled. What may I do for you?"

"You said earlier you'd been speaking to the police inspector, and we wondered if you could share with us what you told him."

"Oh, it wasn't much. He just asked if I'd seen your friend, Dr Shaw, in the lounge and whether I'd served him."

"And had you?"

"I saw him twice while he was here. The first time was before dinner, when I'd served him a vermouth cocktail. Then I saw him later that night when he asked for a brandy."

"Had you met him before he arrived at the hotel?"

"No. He said he was new to Brighton."

Archie studied her. "This cocktail, could you tell us what was in it? Besides the vermouth."

She chuckled. "The inspector asked me that, so I've already checked with the barman. Not the one who was working last night, that was Mr Forshaw, but they all use the same ingredients. Apparently, it was two measures of bourbon, one of vermouth and some orange bitters."

Eliza smiled. "That's very helpful. May I ask how he seemed when you served him?"

Miss Anderson shrugged. "Perfectly normal, on both occasions, although I guessed he'd had a couple of cocktails while he was out. His cheeks were rather rosy." She noticed a gentleman waving to her from across the room. "I'm sorry, I need to go, but that was all the inspector asked about."

"Thank you." Eliza watched her leave. "A cocktail like that would mask the taste and smell of the arsenic, even if the killer had used the dyed version."

Archie nodded. "I'd say so. I wish I'd paid more attention when I sniffed it."

"You weren't to know." Eliza shifted her gaze to Mrs Dunn, who was partway down the lounge, with one of the guests.

"I wonder if the lady Mrs Dunn's with is on her own. They've been talking for a number of minutes now."

Connie followed her gaze. "Isn't that the same woman she was with on Saturday?"

"I'd say so. They're having quite a chat, too."

Connie tutted. "She must have a husband or companion somewhere if she's staying here."

"Not necessarily in this day and age." Eliza grinned at her friend. "Maybe they're talking about the incident. Do you think the police will have spoken to Mrs Dunn yet? She did serve us that first afternoon when David joined us."

"Why don't we ask her?" Mr Bell had beckoned Mrs Dunn over before Eliza could stop him, but there was no smile from her when she arrived.

"I'm not serving these tables. Miss Anderson should be around if you need anything."

Eliza looked up. "Oh, she is, and we've placed our order, but we wondered if we might have a word."

Mrs Dunn scanned the tables further down the room. "Only if it's quick."

"We wanted to ask if the police had spoken to you about one of the guests, Dr Shaw. The man who took afternoon tea with us when we first arrived."

"Dr Shaw?"

"Do you remember him?"

"Oh y-yes ... but I didn't know his name."

"So the police haven't spoken to you?"

"No. Why would they?"

"Unfortunately, Dr Shaw is no longer with us and we'd like to know if you served him at any other time?"

"No. I had no need to. You'll have to speak to Miss Anderson."

"She's already told us she served him a couple of drinks, but we're curious to find out if anyone else had."

"Is that why he's left the hotel, because he had too much to drink?"

Eliza twisted her lips. "You could say that."

"Serves him right, then. Now, I need to get on. Excuse me." She scurried to her end of the room as Eliza turned back to the table, her forehead creased.

"How strange."

Connie looked at her. "What is?"

"That she doesn't know about David's death. She appears to be on very good terms with Miss Anderson, so you'd have expected her to tell her. I'd have told you if the roles were reversed."

"I should hope you would, but why does it matter?"

"I don't know. Does it mean Miss Anderson doesn't want to talk about it?"

Archie shrugged. "She seemed perfectly happy to talk to us."

"Maybe it's nothing, then. I suppose we'd better speak to the barman next. Do you think they'll let us all into the bar area? Or should we ask if the barman can join us here?" She paused as Miss Anderson appeared with a large stand of sandwiches and cake. "Here's someone who can tell us."

Miss Anderson placed the stand on the table. "What may I help with now?"

"We'd like to talk to the barman who was on duty between five and six o'clock last night. Did you say it was Mr Forshaw?"

"Yes, that's right, but he doesn't start until six this evening."

Eliza sighed. "Does he ever venture out of the bar, or might I go in there to speak to him?"

"Oh, no. Ladies are strictly forbidden. Even the waitresses need to use a hatch to place our orders. I could find someone to ask him to come here if you like, but it probably won't be until later tonight."

"All right, thank you. Don't say anything to him for now. We'll think about what we want to do."

Archie accepted the plate Eliza handed to him. "Why don't you let me and your father speak to him? We can go into the bar while you're dressing for dinner."

"We don't have much choice. We'll come up with a list of questions while we drink this tea."

· · ·

Archie and Mr Bell were already in the lounge when Eliza and Connie arrived for their pre-dinner sherry, but Eliza's brow creased.

"That was quick."

"He's a man of few words." Mr Bell's voice was gruff. "He said he'd spoken to the police and he'd nothing else to add."

"Did he tell you what he'd told them?"

Archie shrugged. "It's hard to tell. He just confirmed he'd been in the bar all evening and hadn't tampered with any drinks."

"That was it?"

"We tried to push him, but he said that when the orders come to him, he's no idea who any of them are for, so even if he wished anyone any harm, he wouldn't know which drink to poison."

Mr Bell nodded. "He has a point."

Eliza cocked her head to one side. "He may have asked someone. We'd better check." She looked at Archie. "Did you ask if he'd seen David?"

"He didn't give the impression that he had, which is plausible. As far as we can tell, David didn't go into the bar."

Eliza sighed. "So even if Mr Forshaw knew whose glass was whose, it doesn't look like he had a motive."

"That's what it looks like, but I'm struggling to think why anyone else would have one, either. It makes no sense."

## CHAPTER TEN

E liza and Connie chose a table in the far corner of the lounge, with a good view of the rest of the room, for their after-dinner cup of tea. Eliza smiled as Miss Anderson placed a plate of petits fours beside the teapot.

"They look lovely, thank you."

"Are the gentlemen not joining you tonight?"

"They will later, but they wanted to go into the bar for a snifter first."

"That's not so bad. It's always nice spending time on your own."

"Oh, it is, and we intend to make the most of it." Eliza grinned at Miss Anderson before she turned her attention to the plate of dainty cakes and selected a small square of sponge with a chocolate topping. "I hope this tastes as good as it looks."

Connie used a cake fork to slice through a similar-sized cake covered with lemon icing. "Hmm." She licked her lips. "Mine is."

They sat in silence, enjoying their delights, until a rotund, middle-aged man and his similarly shaped wife arrived at the next table.

"Good evening." The man raised his hat before placing it on the seat beside him. His wife smiled as Eliza dabbed her mouth with a napkin.

"Good evening. If you're waiting for a pot of tea, you're in for a treat."

"We'll look forward to it."

Eliza eyed the last of the cakes, but left it where it was. "I'm Mrs Thomson, and this is my companion, Mrs Appleton. It's nice to meet you."

The man nodded. "Likewise. Mr and Mrs Brooks."

"Have you been at the hotel long?"

"This is the start of our second week."

"You're here for two weeks? How lovely. I hope this police investigation isn't spoiling anything."

Mr Brooks tutted. "It's a trifle inconvenient, but we've already told the police all we know, so hopefully they'll leave us in peace."

"Were you acquainted with Dr Shaw?"

"Not at all, but it turns out we all spent Saturday evening in the same restaurant. The police tracked us down to ask if we could tell them anything about his movements."

"They identified the restaurant, then?"

Mrs Brooks smiled. "It's a place called English's on East Street. It's very nice. Do you know it?"

"No, I can't say we do. This is our first time to Brighton."

"I believe it was the same for poor Dr Shaw. He'd had to ask one of the porters for directions because it was his lady friend who'd suggested the restaurant."

"Lady friend?" Eliza raised an eyebrow, but Mr Brooks interrupted.

"May I ask why you're so interested?"

"Oh, erm ... curiosity, I suppose. Dr Shaw was an old friend of my husband's, so we're keen to find out who'd want to harm him."

Mrs Brooks leaned across the table. "Did you know him well?"

"To be honest, we hadn't seen him for years, but we were hoping to catch up while he was here. He only left the hotel on Saturday because his meeting was a prior engagement, but he didn't mention it was with a lady."

"It must have been a secret assignation, then." Mrs Brooks tittered. "I'd say she was a little younger than him, and rather pretty, with dark hair tied in an elaborate chignon. They seemed rather taken with each other."

"Really?" Eliza's eyes widened.

"They even had a glass of wine each, not that she drank hers. Once Dr Shaw had finished his, she offered it to him."

"She didn't even have a taste?"

Mrs Brooks looked at her husband. "I don't recall seeing her drinking, but I wasn't paying that much attention. Did you notice?"

He shrugged. "Can't say I did."

Eliza's shoulders slumped. "Did you mention that to the police?"

Mrs Brooks's brow furrowed. "I don't think we did, now you ask. We only told them we'd seen him with a young lady."

"Did you catch the lady's name, by any chance?"

"No, we didn't, but I expect the police will find out..."

A voice interrupted them. "This looks interesting. May we join you?"

Eliza grinned at them. "Good evening, Mrs Smith, Mrs Gardener. Of course you may. Have you met Mr and Mrs Brooks?"

"We have now. Good evening."

Mr Brooks stood up. "Please, join us. The more the merrier."

"Thank you." There was a glint in Mrs Smith's eyes as they took their seats. "Do you have any news about what was going on the other day?"

Eliza took a sip of her tea. "Presumably you've heard about Dr Shaw's unfortunate demise."

"No! What have we missed?"

Eliza sighed. "An old friend of ours, Dr Shaw, was found dead in a bathing machine on Sunday morning. That's why the police have been in the hotel."

"Good gracious, how sad. Please accept our condolences."

"Thank you. He wasn't a close friend, but it was still a bit of a shock."

Mrs Smith looked at her sister-in-law. "Do you remember meeting a Dr Shaw?"

Eliza interrupted. "I doubt you would have. He was only in the hotel for a few hours before he was killed."

"What a shame."

Mrs Gardener leaned forward. "What did he look like?"

"Tall and slim, with black hair."

She turned to Mrs Smith. "Didn't we see someone like that in the bar before we went out on Saturday evening?"

"In the lounge?"

"Yes."

"Yes, we did. Sitting near the door drinking a cocktail if I remember rightly."

Eliza raised an eyebrow. "That's very observant."

"I may be old, but I still notice when a man's attractive."

Eliza tried to cover her smirk. "Well, I'm glad you do. Not that we have much more information for you. Mr and Mrs Brooks were just telling us they saw him in a restaurant that evening with a lady."

Mrs Gardener gasped. "On his first evening? That didn't take him long. Out of interest, was he drinking much?"

Mrs Brooks stuttered. "Y-yes, actually, he was. Why?"

"We thought so." She looked at Mrs Smith. "We saw him again when we got back to the hotel later that evening ... after our game of bridge ... and he looked rather worse for wear."

"You saw him later?" Eliza's mouth fell open. "What time would that have been?"

They turned to each other. "Around midnight?"

Mrs Smith nodded. "I would say so."

"Not long before the time of death..." Eliza spoke to no one in particular, but Mrs Gardener gasped.

"How do you know that?"

"My husband was speaking to the police ... he's a doctor and knew Dr Shaw from their time at medical school. Can you remember whether he was inside or outside the hotel when you encountered him?"

"We'd just reached the top of the steps and were expecting the doorman to let us in when a man stumbled through the door and nearly knocked Mrs Smith over. Now I think about it, it was the same man."

"Oh dear." Eliza studied the woman. "Were you hurt?"

"Not at all. I can move faster than you'd expect. Not that

this doctor seemed to notice the way he carried on down the steps."

"Was there anyone waiting for him?"

The ladies looked at each other. "I don't think so."

"Did you see where he went?"

Mrs Smith shook her head. "I'm afraid I didn't. After nearly being knocked over, I was keen to get inside."

"And I wanted to get her inside, too." Mrs Gardener rolled her shoulders. "We have no time for drunkards and I was just glad he'd gone." They paused as Miss Anderson arrived with the Brookses' tea.

"Here you are, sir." She turned to Mrs Smith. "May I get you something?"

"We'll have the same, please."

"Certainly."

Mrs Gardener waited for Miss Anderson to leave before she gestured towards her. "Have you spoken to her about your doctor friend?"

"She didn't seem to know much. She told us she served him with the cocktail he was drinking when you left the hotel, and then with a brandy when he came back that evening. He said it was for an upset stomach..."

Mrs Gardener tutted. "A likely tale. I expect he just wanted an excuse for another drink."

Eliza grimaced at Connie, but turned back to Mrs Smith, who was talking to her.

"Did the waitress tell you why she was having words with the other one, Mrs Dunn? We were in the lounge, but too far away to hear properly. It sounded as if they were arguing about who would serve him."

"Why would they do that?" Eliza's forehead creased. "As

you say, he was rather good-looking. Did they both want to serve him?"

"I don't think so. I'd say neither of them wanted to."

"You're sure? They both said they'd never met him before."

Mrs Smith shrugged. "Maybe they'd spotted he was a bit of a womaniser and wanted to stay away. Or they were concerned about the amount he had to drink."

Eliza puffed out her cheeks. "It's a possibility, although I wasn't aware of that side of him. I'd better ask them."

Mr Brooks's ample moustache twitched. "Shouldn't we leave that to the police?"

"Oh, we will ... and we'll pass on any information we come across in the meantime." She turned to Mrs Smith. "Have you spoken to the police yet?"

"No, they've not asked to see us. Do you think we should approach them?"

Eliza sighed. "Probably. It could be a while before they get around to asking you."

Mr Brooks disturbed them as he got to his feet and waved across the room. "Colonel, over here."

A slim, straight-backed man with a pencil moustache ushered his wife across the room. "Good evening, Mr Brooks. I wasn't sure if we'd be interrupting."

"Not at all. Take a seat. We're talking about this confounded death the police are investigating."

"Ah, that." The colonel accepted Eliza's offer for him and his wife to join their table.

"What do we know?"

"Not a lot, actually. Have the police spoken to you?"

"There's no need. As far as I'm aware, we never set eyes on the chap."

"Oh..." Eliza stopped when all eyes turned on her. "I'm sorry, I must be mistaken. I thought my husband had pointed you out as being in the lounge when Dr Shaw joined them on the night he died."

The colonel's eyes narrowed. "We were in the lounge on Saturday, but only from about a quarter to ten onwards."

"That's right. He said he'd seen you after we'd gone to bed ... which was about half past nine."

The colonel's brow creased. "Where was your husband sitting?"

Eliza hesitated. "I can't say for certain, but if he was where we left him, he was at the table by the window nearest the door."

"The one with the palms?"

"Yes. That's right."

The colonel peered towards the opposite corner of the room as Mrs Giles ventured to speak. "I think I saw a man join that table. My husband was ordering another drink, so was probably distracted. There were two men there when we arrived, one older with grey hair and a moustache, and a younger one with darker colouring. Might that be them?"

"That sounds like them. The man who joined them was tall and slim, with black hair."

"Yes, that was him. It all looked perfectly normal. They were still there when we left."

Eliza sighed. *At least that confirms Archie's alibi.* "That's helpful, thank you. Had you been anywhere nice when you were out?"

The colonel cut back in. "Only for a walk along the promenade and back. To help the digestion..."

Mrs Giles gave a cautious smile. "And we like to admire the view. The beach looks so much tidier of an evening when all the bathing machines are arranged neatly along the back wall."

Eliza grinned. "You noticed the bathing machines?"

Mrs Giles hesitated. "Well, yes. It's difficult not to if you walk on that side of the road."

"And they were all in order? None were still down the beach?"

"No, none at all."

"Were there any people on the beach?"

"I can't be certain, but I doubt it. It was getting dark, and the tide was coming in. You wouldn't want to get caught out down there unawares."

"No, you wouldn't. Thank you, Mrs Giles, that's very helpful."

# CHAPTER ELEVEN

The lounge was emptying out when Archie and Mr Bell joined them, and Mr and Mrs Brooks bid them good evening as they passed on their way to the foyer.

Archie grinned at Eliza. "You look as if you've had quite a party."

"It's been very pleasant." She introduced them to the colonel and his wife, as well as the ladies, before Mrs Smith got to her feet.

"It's nice to meet you, Dr Thomson, but I'm afraid it's time for us to go to bed, too. We've had a couple of late nights recently and it does tend to catch up with us."

"It does indeed." He gave a slight bow. "Sleep well."

Colonel Giles stood up and offered Archie his chair. "Forgive us for taking your seats."

"Not at all. I'm glad my wife and her companion had company."

"It's been rather jolly to tell you the truth, but we'll leave you for now. We don't want to outstay our welcome."

"You'd be doing nothing of the sort."

"That's nice of you to say, but we'll take our leave, regardless. Perhaps I may join you in the bar one evening."

"Absolutely. I'll look out for you."

Eliza grinned at Archie. "Do you always have that effect?"

He laughed. "I can't help it. Have you had a productive evening?"

"I've no idea what you mean."

Archie raised an eyebrow. "Don't tell me you sat with all those people and didn't mention David's death once."

Connie tittered. "It was quite informative. People see all sorts of things, yet don't realise what's relevant."

"What sort of things?"

"Well, for one–" Eliza lowered her voice "–the person David met on Saturday night was a lady!"

"Really! The dark horse. Do we know who she is?"

Her shoulders slumped. "No, but Mrs Brooks said she was very pretty."

"I don't doubt it, knowing David. How do they know about her?"

"They were in the same restaurant, so the police tracked them down..." Eliza looked around as Miss Anderson arrived by her side.

"Good evening, gentlemen. I wasn't sure if I'd see you in here tonight."

Mr Bell grinned. "We couldn't stay away for long. My daughter would have missed us, eventually."

"I'd be wondering how many brandies you'd consumed, more like..." She cocked her head to one side. "Actually, Miss Anderson, while you're here, may I ask you a couple of questions?"

"Yes, we're quiet enough now. What would you like to know?"

"The barman, Mr Forshaw, does he ever enquire who the drinks are for when you take an order?"

"Not from me. He never has a lot of time, so just gets on with it."

"And that was the case last Saturday?"

"I don't remember him being any different. You don't think he slipped the poison into a drink, do you?"

"Not at the moment, but I wanted to check."

"Ah, good. I don't want to be worrying about him poisoning me."

Eliza chuckled. "I doubt he would."

"You're probably right. Will that be all?"

"Actually, no. We heard that you and Mrs Dunn had a bit of a disagreement on Saturday about who served Dr Shaw. Is that true?"

"What ... who told you that?"

"Nobody with any certainty, but I wanted to ask to make sure they weren't mistaken."

Miss Anderson sighed. "No, they weren't. It was down to Mrs Dunn, really. She'd served the gentleman when he first came into the lounge, but as soon as she'd taken his order, she asked if I'd take over. I wasn't happy because he wasn't at one of my tables, but in the end we swapped our whole allocation so I served him when he next came in. Not that I saw much of him..."

"No." Eliza's forehead creased. "Why wouldn't Mrs Dunn want to serve him?"

Miss Anderson shrugged. "Apparently, he said something she didn't like."

"What did he say?" Eliza glanced around the table. "We were sitting with him, but I didn't hear him say anything untoward."

"Maybe we should ask Mrs Dunn–" Mr Bell studied the room "–not that I can see her."

Miss Anderson bit her lip. "I hope I've not said anything out of turn."

"Not at all. We need to understand what happened, so if we can discount bits of information like this, it's a great help for the police."

"I see." Miss Anderson scanned the room. "Mrs Dunn must have finished for the evening. She usually leaves at around ten o'clock unless we're busy."

"Never mind. It's not urgent. We'll catch her tomorrow."

After ordering a nightcap for himself and Mr Bell, and hot chocolate drinks for the ladies, Archie sat back in his chair and smiled at Connie. "Are you all ready for tomorrow?"

Her cheeks coloured. "I am, although it won't feel right leaving Eliza on her own with this investigation going on."

"It wouldn't surprise me if Sergeant Cooper wants to help. You could do with having a list of things you'd like to know."

Eliza huffed. "I'm perfectly capable of finding them out myself."

"We all know you are, but there are times when it helps to have a policeman in uniform, even if he isn't officially assigned to the investigation."

Connie nudged her. "We could get him to find out what the local police are up to. They're not likely to tell us."

"That's true, although I'm not sure Inspector Jarvis will

DEATH BY THE SEA

tell Sergeant Cooper if he knows he's with us. Don't forget, we're still down as possible suspects."

Connie sighed. "He could speak to the constable. If Constable Jenkins in Moreton is anything to go by, they like to show off with what they know."

Archie chuckled. "She has a point."

Eliza nodded. "We could also see if we can find out where the arsenic came from ... and if they're any closer to finding out who wrote the letter. Nobody else I've spoken to has mentioned they've had their handwriting checked."

Connie grinned. "I'm sure he'll be pleased to be involved. He was rather nervous about joining us."

Eliza gasped. "He's known us for years."

"This is different. We're in a smart hotel, for one thing, and he's never travelled so far from Moreton before. You will be gentle with him, won't you?"

"Of course we will. I'd no idea." Eliza turned to Archie. "Maybe you could take him to the bar before luncheon to settle him down."

Archie nodded. "Only if he's already spoken to the police. We don't want them seeing us together."

Eliza looked at Connie. "What time is he arriving?"

"He's catching the first train, so should be here for ten o'clock."

"Splendid. We'll have to get him to work straight away."

Connie's face twisted as Eliza spoke.

"What's the matter? Have you made other plans?"

"No, it's Mrs Dunn." Connie pointed across the lounge. "Miss Anderson said she'd finished for the day."

Eliza swivelled in her seat to see the waitress carrying a tray along the far end of the room. "What's she doing here?"

"Maybe Miss Anderson was mistaken."

"You'd think she'd know. I wonder if she'll talk to us."

"We can only try." Mr Bell stood up. "I'll go and ask her nicely."

"No, wait. Miss Anderson will be here with our drinks in a minute. Wait until she's been and gone."

Mrs Dunn had moved to the entrance to the foyer by the time their drinks had been delivered, and Mr Bell strode the length of the lounge to speak to her. After a brief conversation, he escorted her across the room and Eliza smiled when she arrived.

"Thank you for joining us. Miss Anderson told us you'd finished for the evening."

"I didn't think I'd sleep after everything that's happened, so I took a break and came back."

"Do you usually do that?"

"We don't usually have guests murdered."

"Oh..."

Mrs Dunn's cheeks coloured. "I'm sorry, but I'm unsettled by what's happened. My husband will be working until midnight, and given I've nothing to go home for, I decided to wait and walk with him."

"That's understandable. Does your husband often work late?"

She nodded. "It's usually about eleven or twelve o'clock. He doesn't mind, though. It means he doesn't have to get out of bed so early in the morning. Is that what you wanted to ask me?"

"Oh, no. I was just interested. The thing we were wondering is why you didn't want to serve Dr Shaw that first night he was in the hotel."

She took a step backwards. "How did you know?"

"Some guests overheard you talking with Miss Anderson, but it struck us as strange, given you told us you didn't know him."

"And I don't ... didn't..."

"Then why didn't you want to serve him?"

She shrugged but continued when Eliza remained silent.

"If you must know, he said something that upset me."

"Do you mind me asking what?"

Mrs Dunn stared at the floor. "No, but ... well, I don't remember now. I think I overreacted because I'd been talking to my mother for longer than I should have been, and was worried he'd noticed."

"Your mother? Was she the lady I saw you talking to earlier?"

"Possibly. She's come to Brighton for a visit, but can't afford to stay in a hotel like this. She's taken lodgings in a guest house on the other side of the Grand Hotel, but comes here for afternoon tea. I can't ignore her."

"That must be hard, not being able to spend time together. When did you last see her?"

"Not since I left London at the start of the season."

"So, nearly six months?"

Mrs Dunn nodded. "Me and my husband are happy here, but I do miss her. I'm trying to persuade her to move herself, but she's not made up her mind. All her friends are in London."

"I can understand that. Well, thank you, Mrs Dunn, we'll let you get on."

Connie watched her go. "Do you believe her?"

"I believe she was telling the truth about her mother and

that she'd been talking for too long. Do I think David upset her?" She looked at Archie. "What would you say? We were with him when he ordered. Did you hear anything to suggest he had?"

Archie shrugged. "I can't say I did, but I probably wasn't paying much attention. I only remember him asking for another cup and saucer so he could share our tea, although why he didn't order a selection of sandwiches for himself, I don't know."

"I decided he didn't want to pay for it."

"That sounds about right." Archie laughed as Connie screwed up her forehead.

"He said how nice it was to be in Brighton after years in London and marvelled at the view of the sea."

Eliza nodded. "He did, but that shouldn't have upset her."

"Maybe it's because she wants her mother to move down here but she won't." Connie pursed her lips. "Or she may have been upset at how excited Dr Shaw was."

"And she may have been emotional at seeing her mother after so long. It can't be easy."

Mr Bell took a sip of his brandy. "Whatever it was, it's probably irrelevant now. The fact she didn't serve Dr Shaw anything other than a cup and saucer suggests she's not our poisoner."

"You're right." She turned back to Archie. "Did you watch Mr Forshaw at work while you were in the bar?"

"We did, and he did exactly what Miss Anderson said. The waiters leave their orders on the bar, and the waitresses use a hatch in the wall. He clearly has a system and deals with everything without troubling anyone."

Eliza huffed. "So even if the police get round to testing the bar for traces of arsenic, I can't see that he'd have a motive or the opportunity to poison David."

Archie shook his head. "That's certainly what it looks like."

# CHAPTER TWELVE

The police were in the foyer when they arrived for breakfast the following morning, but Inspector Jarvis appeared determined to ignore them until he spotted Connie.

"Mrs Appleton, a word, if I may."

Eliza kept hold of Connie's arm as the two of them approached. "Not you, Mrs Thomson. Don't you have breakfast to order?"

"We do that together. Otherwise it arrives separately..."

"Then delay the waitress..."

"If it's all the same to you, Inspector, I'd rather stay with my companion. She's not used to being questioned by the police."

"If she's done nothing wrong, she's nothing to worry about."

"I've done nothing wrong, but it hasn't helped me." She glared at him. "If you'd like to talk to Mrs Appleton, would you be so kind as to do it now?"

"I need to speak to her on her own at some point."

"Not without a chaperone."

He pursed his lips, before turning to Connie. "I need you to write out the following text. You can sit at the table here."

Connie looked at Eliza.

"Don't worry, it won't take long."

Connie accepted the seat the inspector held out for her and picked up the fountain pen as Eliza spoke to the inspector.

"Can I presume you haven't found anyone with handwriting to match the letter?"

"We're still collecting samples."

"And how many do you have so far?"

Inspector Jarvis's back straightened. "That's confidential information."

Eliza sighed. "A word of advice. Just because a woman appeared to write the letter doesn't mean a woman killed him."

His nostrils flared. "Men don't use poison."

"And women don't wheel bathing machines down the beach unaided. Don't forget, Dr Shaw died of drowning."

"He may have helped move the machine..."

"In the state he was in..." Eliza gasped as Connie stood up.

"Here. Will that do?"

The inspector glanced at the paper. "Yes. Thank you. Enjoy your breakfast."

"We will." Eliza glared at the inspector as she took Connie's arm and pulled her towards the dining room. "What a horrible man."

Archie and Mr Bell were waiting by the door, and once they joined them, the maitre d' led them to their table.

Eliza took her seat near the window while Connie sat beside her, with Archie and Mr Bell opposite.

"Did he only want a handwriting sample?"

"For now. He said he wanted to speak to her alone at some point, presumably to ask if I'd put her up to anything, but her handwriting was so different to the original letter, he may have to rethink that. It hasn't crossed his mind that if he asks the killer for a sample of writing, they're highly likely to change it from what was in the letter. I doubt they'll be naïve enough to use the same script."

Archie grinned at her. "I'm surprised you didn't tell him."

"And give him another reason to suspect me. I don't think so."

Mr Bell laughed. "Nobody could ever take you for a fool. Did you get anything else out of him?"

"No, he won't talk to me. Hopefully, the constable will talk to Sergeant Cooper when he arrives." Eliza straightened a napkin across her lap. "It's rather fortunate they're here this morning. Then it will look like Sergeant Cooper just happened upon them."

Mr Bell sat back as a waitress put a pot of tea on the table and he waited until she'd gone. "Are you meeting him at the railway station?"

"We were going to wait for him here. Why?"

"If you want him to speak to the constable, you'll have to tell him what's happened and what you need to know. You can't do that here, if the police are around."

"That's a good point." Eliza looked at Connie. "It can't be much more than a ten- minute walk to the railway station. We could go there after breakfast and wait for him."

Connie hesitated. "It won't look too forward?"

"Connie Appleton!" Eliza rolled her eyes. "You've been walking out together for over a year now. Nothing about your behaviour is forward."

Connie's cheeks flushed. "Very well, then. We've over an hour yet, so we'll be in good time."

The station office felt cold and dark after the bright sunshine outside, and Archie checked his pocket watch once he'd studied the timetable.

"The train I expect him to be on should be here in ten minutes, so we may as well take a seat."

Connie edged to the door. "We won't miss him, will we? He'll have no need to come in here once he gets off the train."

"There are seats on the platform if you prefer."

"And end up covered in soot?" Eliza shuddered. "I'd rather stand outside. We'll hear the train arriving from there."

"All right..." Archie glanced round "...although, we may be better splitting up. You stand by the side door, and we'll go to the main entrance."

Eliza nodded. "Good idea. We'll be closer to the platform then, as well."

By the time they'd taken up their positions, they only had a couple of minutes to wait, and Connie wandered back and forth, peering along the platform as she passed. On her fifth walk past, she stopped.

"It's here."

Eliza joined her as a whistle sounded, and the slow chug of the steam engine drew closer until, with a final release of steam from the engine, the train stopped.

Connie's face was pale. "I hope he didn't miss it."

"Don't look so worried. I expect he'd worked out his timings."

"He'd done that before I left. I'm just nervous. I'll be fine once he arrives. And when I know he's in his uniform. What if he's decided not to wear it?"

Eliza shook her head. "Given that police officers have to wear their uniforms whether they're on duty or not, I doubt Sergeant Cooper owns a normal suit."

Connie chuckled. "You're probably right. Oh, look ... here he is. In his uniform, too."

Connie waved from her place at the end of the platform, causing Sergeant Cooper to break into a broad grin.

"My dear. What an unexpected pleasure when we'd agreed to meet at the hotel."

She beamed like a schoolgirl. "We decided to meet you here instead. There's been a bit of trouble and we wanted to tell you about it before we get to the hotel."

"Trouble?" The smile disappeared from his face. "Are you all right?"

"Yes, I'm fine. It's just that when we arrived, Dr Thomson bumped into an old friend from medical school, but the next morning, he was found dead on the beach. Murdered."

"No!" Sergeant Cooper's eyes widened as he stared at Eliza. "Is Dr Thomson all right?"

"He is, thank you. The problem we have is that the police inspector in charge of the case has me and my husband down as suspects."

"He suspects you?"

Eliza nodded. "I'm afraid so. Dr Thomson's waiting by the other exit with Father, in case we missed you here. Why don't we walk around and meet them, then we can tell you all about it?"

They'd reached the promenade by the time they'd recounted all they knew, and Archie ushered them across the road towards the sea wall. Once they stepped onto the footpath, Sergeant Cooper paused to admire the view and the bathing machines.

"Who'd have thought something like murder could happen in a place like this? It all looks so jolly."

Mr Bell sighed. "It usually is, that's why I chose to come here, but these things happen."

"What would you like me to do?"

Eliza opened her handbag and produced a sheet of paper. "We've found out most of what we've told you by ourselves, but there are still questions. The police probably have some answers that they won't share with us, so we wondered if you could offer your assistance and find out what they know."

He unfolded the paper and stared at the list. "I'm only here for the day. I doubt I could be much help, even if they want to involve me."

"That's not important. In fact, I'm sure Mrs Appleton would prefer it if they didn't need you, but offering your services may be the best way into the conversation."

He nodded. "Very well. Now, what do you want to know?" His eyes flickered as he scanned the list. "Whether they've found the source of the arsenic, or any traces of arsenic in the hotel or restaurant; who Dr Shaw's companion was in the restaurant, and where she lives. Any more information about the letter in Dr Shaw's room. Anything else they may have found out." He puffed out his cheeks. "That's quite a list. What's this letter about?"

"That's rather interesting. On the evening Dr Shaw was poisoned, someone pushed a letter under his door asking to meet him outside the hotel at midnight. They're collecting samples of people's handwriting to check for matches, but we don't know how far they've got."

Connie clung to his arm. "I had to copy out the letter this morning."

"You!" Sergeant Cooper gasped. "They can't possibly believe you had anything to do with it?"

Eliza sighed. "They've no idea what they're doing. They asked me the first time they spoke to me, but my writing was nothing like the letter. Connie's worried they may think I asked her to write it for me."

His eyes narrowed. "You didn't...?"

"Of course not, but the letter may be the key to the murder, so they need to work out who sent it."

Sergeant Cooper only looked vaguely reassured. "Did Dr Shaw leave the hotel at midnight?"

"Yes, but we don't know what happened between then and when he turned up in the bathing machine the following morning."

"Someone definitely pushed the letter under the door? The dinner companion couldn't have handed it to him?"

Eliza stared straight ahead. "I suppose she could, but it's not likely given she was already with him. Why ask to meet again?"

"Maybe the police just assumed it was under the door. It could have got there in any manner of ways."

Connie's eyes sparkled. "We hadn't thought of that. Will you find out for us?"

He stroked the edge of her hand. "It won't be easy, but seeing you asked so nicely."

"Right." Eliza gave a gentle cough to distract them. "We obviously don't want the police knowing you're with us, Sergeant Cooper, so would you care to go on ahead? The hotel's a little further up the road on the right-hand side. I expect you'll find the police in the foyer or in the bar."

He looked at Archie. "Where will I find that?"

"Go through the archway in the far left-hand corner of the foyer and it's the first door on the right. The smoking room is the second door. There's a chance you'll find them in there."

"And some of them are in uniform?"

Connie nodded. "There's a young-looking constable, who we're hoping is keen to share what he knows."

"Splendid, I'll start with him. Once I'm finished, where will I find you?"

Eliza pursed her lips. "I noticed Mr Topham, the doorman, was on the early shift today, so I'd like to speak to him on the way in and possibly any porters who may have been working on Saturday night. Shall we go to the lounge when we're finished? We'll try to sit by the window nearest the door."

The sergeant looked again at Archie for directions.

"The lounge is through the first arch on the same side as the bar. We'll take the nearest available table if the one in the window is occupied."

Sergeant Cooper stood up straight and clicked his heels together. "Right you are. I'll see you shortly."

Connie watched him leave. "He's so brave doing this by himself."

Eliza smirked as she linked her friend's arm. "He'll be fine. He's only speaking to another police officer. Now, shall the rest of us split up? Connie and I will be better speaking to the doorman on our own, rather than the four of us, so shall we go last?"

"Very well. Perhaps I'll wander to the bar with your father to see what's going on."

Mr Topham held open the door for them when they returned to the hotel, but he studied Eliza as she stepped through and stopped beside him.

"May I help?"

She gave him her best smile. "I hope so. I've a couple of questions about Dr Shaw, the man who was unfortunately..."

"Yes, I'm aware who he is. The police have been questioning me every day since the incident happened."

"Really? What have they been asking?"

"Nothing of any consequence, just the timings of his coming and goings, and whether he was always alone."

Eliza cocked her head to one side. "Haven't you already told them that?"

"I have. Why they can't read their notes, I don't know. They've asked so many times, I could say it by rote. The doctor arrived at the hotel at four o'clock on Saturday and left again at quarter past six. He came back shortly after ten, and went out around midnight ... and then I headed for home." The man's face was red. "Forgive me for being so indiscreet, but I needed to get that off my chest. It's as if they think I had something to do with his death and it's very unsettling."

Eliza gave a sympathetic smile. "I'm sure it is. My guess is that they don't know what happened, so they suspect everyone. I imagine Dr Shaw's companion must have had quite a grilling."

Mr Topham studied her. "I can't help you there. I only ever saw him on his own, other than when he was with our porter, Mr Dunn. He helped him several times, but the way the police have been pestering him, he's beginning to wish he hadn't. He's been getting the same questions as me."

"Oh dear. I'd hoped to speak to him myself. Do you think he'll mind if we ask him any more?"

Mr Topham opened the door as several more guests arrived. "He's taking it better than I am, so you can try but don't tell him I sent you."

A small queue was waiting at the porters' desk when Eliza and Connie approached, and they joined the back behind an elderly lady in a fox-fur stole. Eliza groaned. *Just watch her have five bags she needs help with.* She noticed the clock on the wall and leaned over to Connie. "We'll be missing elevenses at this rate."

"Do you want to come back? We may have more questions once we hear from Sergeant Cooper."

"Why not? He's come all this way to visit you, and you've hardly said two words to him."

Archie and Mr Bell were at the table by the window when they walked into the lounge, and they both stood up to help with the chairs.

"Is there no sign of Sergeant Cooper?"

Archie grinned. "He was in the bar talking to the

constable when we saw him, so we left him to it. We didn't want to put him off."

"Well, let's hope he won't be long. Should we order morning coffee for him?"

"I would say so. It looked like the police were tidying up, so he shouldn't be long. Did you learn anything useful from the doorman?"

"Not really. He confirmed the times of David's comings and goings, but said he never saw him with anyone else."

"So he met the lady in question at the restaurant and presumably walked her home?"

"I imagine so. We shouldn't be surprised. We know he didn't bring her here for a nightcap."

Connie fixed her eyes on the door. "All the more reason to hope Sergeant Cooper has had some joy with the police. We'll never find her on our own."

Eliza put a hand on her friend's. "If the police can find her, then we can, too. It will just take time. The problem is, we're going to run out of that if we're not careful."

Connie's face suddenly brightened. "He's here now." She gazed at Sergeant Cooper as he approached. "How did you get on?"

"I got some answers for you, if that's what you mean. Should we take a walk, in case the inspector comes in here? I don't want to be found out."

Eliza nodded. "Do you mind if I come with you, for the first few minutes at least? We've not ordered coffee yet."

"Not at all."

Eliza grinned at Archie as she stood up. "Would you order coffee for me? I won't be long."

# CHAPTER THIRTEEN

Sergeant Cooper waited for Eliza and Connie to take a seat on the promenade before he perched on the edge of the bench nearest Connie.

Eliza leaned across her friend. "Were they happy to talk to you?"

"The constable was. You were right. It's his first murder investigation and he couldn't wait to talk to someone. I gave him a few lines of enquiry to drop into the investigation, too, so hopefully he'll be happy to speak to me again if I see him."

"Splendid." Eliza grinned at her friend. "Did he answer all our questions?"

"Most of them." He pulled the piece of paper from his pocket. "Let me see. Have they found the source of the arsenic? No, not yet. The constable's been to every store in Brighton, but nobody who registered a purchase can be traced to the Metropole."

"Hmm. Where did it come from, then?"

"At the moment, they're out of ideas. They did find traces

of arsenic around the bar area in the hotel, so they're hoping to use it to find out if it was white arsenic or if it had the added dye. All the stores sold the dyed variety, so if it's white stuff, it will send the search in a different direction."

"Yes, it will. It will also confirm that the poisoning took place here and not in the restaurant." Eliza looked at Sergeant Cooper. "Unless they found any in the restaurant."

"The constable didn't mention it, so either they've not checked, or they didn't."

Connie studied her. "So it's likely that the woman he had dinner with had nothing to do with it?"

"Not unless she was working with someone else. She wouldn't be allowed into the bar, for one thing. Even if she'd given him a second dose in the restaurant, she'd have had to be careful adding it to the glass, assuming she had the opportunity."

Sergeant Cooper sighed. "That's a shame, because the police have found her. A Miss Young, apparently, who lives at an address on Freshfield Road."

"Really! Have they spoken to her?"

"Not yet. The constable said the inspector was planning to go early this afternoon."

"Perhaps we should still speak to her. She may have some information that helps."

She made a note of the address and turned back to the sergeant. "What about the letter?"

Sergeant Cooper scratched his head. "That's a strange one. They sent it to the laboratory to check if it had any arsenic on it, and they've not had it back. Without the letter, they've been unable to check the handwriting against any of the samples they've collected."

"Did they say how many people they'd asked?"

"No, and I'm afraid I didn't ask."

Eliza huffed. "That was my fault. I didn't put it on the list of questions."

"If I get another chance, I'll check for you."

"Thank you, Sergeant. It would be interesting to find out if they're asking everyone, or just those they suspect could be the killer. When they spoke to me, they were of the impression it had been written by a woman, but I'm struggling with the idea that anyone other than a burly man could move a bathing machine down the beach on their own."

"Maybe there was more than one person involved."

Eliza nodded. "That wouldn't surprise me." She paused and glanced out towards the sea. "Did they say anything else of interest? Any more suspects we've not thought of?"

"No, they're at something of a loss. They've not come up with a motive, either."

"That makes me feel better that we've not found one." She stood up. "Right, I'll give you two a little time to yourselves. Will you join us for luncheon?"

Connie nodded. "Oh, yes. If you don't mind."

"Of course I don't. I'll meet you in the lounge at five to one."


The foyer had emptied by the time Eliza returned to the hotel, and as soon as she saw Mr Dunn on his own, she scurried to the porters' desk. He smiled as she approached.

"May I help, madam?"

"I hope so. Do you mind if I ask you a couple of questions?"

The smile fell from his face as he took a step backwards. "Not about this murder ... I've already told the police everything..."

"I'm sure you have, but if you wouldn't mind telling me, too. My husband was a friend of Dr Shaw, and the police are being far too selective about what they're sharing with us. If I could put his mind at rest..."

His eyes scanned the foyer. "Very well. What would you like to know?"

"We're keen to find out what Dr Shaw did while he was here, and understand you spoke to him on several occasions."

"I did, but not about anything of interest. The first time was when I welcomed him to the hotel and took his bags to the room. He didn't join me because he wanted to go straight into the lounge when he arrived."

"That would be when he met us." Eliza studied him. "Out of interest, when you were in his room, did you notice a letter waiting for him? Or possibly deliver one with his bags?"

"No, I can't say I did. Not that I did any prying, you understand. I placed his bags on the ottoman then left."

"And once you came downstairs, did you see him again that afternoon?"

"When he left the lounge, he wanted directions to English's restaurant on East Street, which I provided."

"Do you know if he walked to the restaurant or took a carriage?"

"Oh, he walked. It's only ten minutes away."

"What about after that?"

"That was the last I saw of him. I finished work at eleven that evening and then wasn't in again until three the following afternoon, by which time they'd found his body."

"Yes, that's right." Eliza glanced behind her at the queue. "I'd better let you get on. Thank you, Mr Dunn. That was very helpful."

A tall silver coffee pot sat in the middle of the table when Eliza got to the lounge, and once she'd settled herself in her chair, she poured herself a cup and topped it up with milk.

"I hope it's not gone cold." She took a sip. "No, it's fine. Thank goodness. I needed that."

Archie waited as she sat back. "How did Sergeant Cooper get on?"

"Very well. They found evidence of arsenic in the bar, which suggests the poisoning took place here."

"Do we know who bought it?"

"No. Apparently, they've been around all the stores and chemists, but nobody connected with the hotel has bought any."

Mr Bell leaned forward, his elbows on his knees. "What do we do now?"

"The police have found the woman David had dinner with, and I have an address, so I thought we could speak to her. She almost certainly had nothing to do with the poisoning, because there are no accounts of her being in the hotel, but she may have seen something." She looked at Archie. "What time is it?"

He checked his pocket watch. "Nearly quarter to twelve."

"Hmm. We probably don't have time to go before luncheon. We'll go this afternoon."

"Who's we?" Archie gave her a quizzical look. "Connie

will be preoccupied while Sergeant Cooper is here. Do you want me and your father to speak to her?"

Eliza took a sip of her coffee. "She probably won't talk so freely if you're with me, but you can walk me to the house and I'll visit her myself. We can't waste a day..."

Archie shook his head. "No. You may think it's unlikely, but she's a potential killer, so I don't want you being on your own with her. I'll tell you what, why don't you invite her here for afternoon tea? If you write a letter now, explaining who you are and why you'd like to speak to her, we could get a bellboy to deliver it."

Eliza's forehead creased. "What if she doesn't come?"

"Then we'll think of something else."

Eliza nodded. "All right. It will give me time to decide what to ask her when she gets here."

Connie and Sergeant Cooper were in the lounge with Mr Bell when Eliza returned from writing her letter in the library.

"Am I late?"

Connie giggled. "No, we're a bit early. We walked along the pier and when we got back to the promenade, there wasn't time to go anywhere else. Besides, neither of us has had a drink since breakfast, so we've ordered some lemonade."

Sergeant Cooper offered Eliza his seat. "You sit here. I want to check the police aren't still in the hotel. I'd hate them to stumble across us."

"Good idea. I didn't see them on my travels, but we can't be too careful."

Mr Bell stood up. "I'll stretch my legs, too. I've been sitting down for too long. What did you do with Archie?"

Eliza scanned the room. "He went to the porters' desk with the letter. There must be a queue."

Mr Bell smirked. "Either that or he got lost on the way here and ended up in the bar. I'll go and find him."

Connie gazed at Sergeant Cooper as he strode towards the foyer ahead of Mr Bell. "It was lovely on the pier. It made such a change to walking around Moreton."

"I imagine it did. You should do it more often when Sergeant Cooper has a day off."

Connie's face fell. "What about you?"

"I think I can manage every now and again. Have you made any plans for this afternoon?"

"Not really, but I can't say I'm sorry. Mr Bell told us you're hoping to take afternoon tea with Miss Young."

"That's the plan. I've suggested she come here at four o'clock, so that at least Archie and Father will be around if there's any trouble."

Connie's forehead creased. "What sort of trouble?"

"I don't know. It's just Archie being cautious. He didn't want me to be on my own with her."

"But I'd be with you."

"We thought you'd like to spend time with Sergeant Cooper before he has to leave again."

Connie fell silent. "I would like to be with him, but I want to help you, too. We're planning to take a walk in the opposite direction after luncheon, but I'd like to join you for afternoon tea."

"Splendid! I'd hoped you would ... but what will you do with Sergeant Cooper?"

"He'll be happy to sit with Dr Thomson for a while. If he doesn't mind."

"Of course he won't, and it will make me feel better having you with me. Now, we need to decide what we're going to ask her."

# CHAPTER FOURTEEN

As four o'clock approached, Eliza and Connie found a table near the centre of the lounge and took their seats. Connie gave a discreet wave to Sergeant Cooper, who was at the table by the window with Archie and Mr Bell.

"He seems settled enough."

"He'll be fine. I just hope Miss Young joins us."

"What does she look like?"

"I'm not sure. Mrs Brooks described her as being young and pretty and when they saw her, she wore her hair in an elaborate chignon. I doubt she'll go to the same trouble for us, but hopefully she'll still be recognisable. I suggested in the letter that she ask one of the staff to show her to our table. Most of them know us by now."

Connie gulped. "Could that be her?" She nodded towards the archway where Mr Dunn stood with a young lady surveying the room.

"I would say so ... although she's not as young as I was expecting." Eliza stood up and waved before Mr Dunn brought their guest over.

"A Miss Young to see you, ladies."

Eliza smiled at them both. "Thank you, Mr Dunn. Please, take a seat, Miss Young. I'm Mrs Thomson, and this is my companion, Mrs Appleton."

"Pleased to meet you." Her hands visibly shook as Mr Dunn pulled out a chair for her. "You said you needed my help?"

"I did, but before we get to that, I'm about to order afternoon tea. Would you care to join us?"

Miss Young eyed the impressive chandeliers hanging from the ceiling. "That would be lovely. I've never had the chance to dine here before."

"Then I hope you enjoy it."

Miss Young sat in silence as Miss Anderson joined them and took their order, before Eliza settled back in her seat.

"I'm sorry to write to you out of the blue, but, as I said in my letter, my husband and I were acquaintances of Dr Shaw and we're keen to find out what happened to him on Saturday evening."

Miss Young wiped a tear from the corner of her eye. "It was such a shock."

"It was. Did you know him well?"

"Well enough..."

When she failed to elaborate, Eliza continued. "Unfortunately, the police don't seem to be making much headway and we leave Brighton this coming weekend, so we'd like to hurry them along. Have they visited you yet?"

"An Inspector Jarvis called earlier with some of his uniformed men."

"Did he have much to say?"

"Not really. He didn't even express any condolences. All

he was interested in was whether I had any rat poison, which I didn't. Not that they believed me until they'd searched every cupboard and checked the surfaces for arsenic."

"Did they ask you about a letter?"

"A letter? No. Who was it from?"

"It wasn't signed, but whoever wrote it wanted to speak to Dr Shaw. They asked him to meet them outside the hotel at midnight. Did he mention it to you?"

"No, not a word."

Eliza huffed. "That's frustrating."

"The constable asked for a sample of my handwriting. Does that mean they think I sent it?"

"I wouldn't jump to conclusions. We've had to do the same. They need to find out who wrote the letter, so they'll be getting handwriting samples from a number of women to compare them to the original."

"They think it was a woman?"

"It looked like a woman's handwriting, so that's the line they're pursuing. It's difficult to argue with them, but I did point out that the letter writer may not be the killer."

Miss Young straightened her back. "Well, I can assure you I didn't write it ... or poison David. Why would I when I'd only seen him hours earlier?"

"They won't have considered that when they spoke to you." Eliza cocked her head to one side. "Did they ask much about Dr Shaw?"

"Only if he'd been ill during dinner."

"And had he?"

"A little. He complained of an upset stomach when he first arrived, but put it down to being hungry. He said he felt better by the end of the evening and was happy enough when we took a walk afterwards."

Eliza pursed her lips. "I'm sorry to be indiscreet, but I presume he walked you home. When you arrived, did you invite him in?"

"Gracious, no. He was a friend I hadn't seen for several years, nothing more than that. We had a nice evening and said we must do it again, but obviously, it wasn't meant to be."

"A little like us. I hadn't seen him for nearly twenty years before he turned up at the hotel, although he had bumped into my husband on several occasions. The two of them were at medical school together, and there were several years when we spent a lot of time socialising." She waited as Miss Anderson arrived with a pot of tea and a stand full of sweet and savoury treats.

"Here we are, ladies." She unloaded everything from her tray. "I hope you enjoy it."

Eliza indicated to the delicate triangular sandwiches. "Please, help yourself."

Miss Young took a single sandwich but laid it on her plate. "Are you from London?"

"In a manner of speaking. I lived there for many years, including when my husband was starting out, but a few years ago we moved back to my childhood village of Moreton, which is on the outskirts."

"I expect Dr Shaw was too busy to keep in touch once your husband left London."

"It was when they left medical school that we drifted apart. I suppose we were all busy at the time. How did you become friendly with him?"

"I used to live in London, too. I was a nurse and worked in Dr Shaw's department."

"Do you still work?"

"No. I had to give it up when I moved to Brighton. Mother has suffered with her chest for as long as I can remember, but it got so bad, the doctor suggested she move down here for the clean air. She did well to start with, but she can't take care of herself any more, so I moved to be with her."

"She's fortunate she has you, especially with your nursing background."

"I'm only doing what anyone would do."

Eliza picked up a cucumber sandwich. "Did Dr Shaw say why he moved down here?"

"Oh, no... He was more interested in finding out about Brighton. He was very excited to be near the sea."

"He was certainly enamoured by the view from the hotel when we saw him, but was that a good enough reason to move? I don't suppose we'll ever find out now."

"No. He'll have taken his secret with him."

Eliza raised an eyebrow. "Secret?"

"Oh! All I meant was that he didn't tell anyone why he was here."

"Ah." She paused as Miss Young took a bite from her sandwich. "Another thing that's been puzzling me is who knew him well enough to want him dead when he'd only just arrived in Brighton? Did he have any acquaintances here besides you?"

"N-no. I-I don't think so." The colour drained from Miss Young's cheeks. "You think I did it, don't you? Is that why you've invited me here for this fancy tea...?"

"Not at all. We just want to understand what happened to Dr Shaw."

Tears welled in Miss Young's eyes. "I've told you I had no access to rat poison, and the police found no traces of arsenic at the house or the restaurant."

Eliza glanced at Connie. "They've tested the restaurant?"

"That's what they said, so I presumed they thought I was innocent..."

Eliza held up her hands. "Please, Miss Young, don't upset yourself. I didn't mean to imply anything. We've already heard that the poison was most likely added to his drink in the hotel, not the restaurant."

"I've never set foot in this hotel before today..." Her eyes were wide as she stared at the two of them.

"We know that."

"That was one of the reasons I accepted your invitation, so I could see what it's like..." She stopped. "You know?"

"That you weren't in the hotel on Saturday, yes. Not with Dr Shaw, at any rate. The doorman and porter have both confirmed he was alone whenever they saw him. We also believe the arsenic was added to his drinks in the bar area, where ladies aren't allowed."

Miss Young's forehead creased. "Then why am I here?"

"Because you were the person he spent the most time with while he was here. We thought he might have said something to suggest why anyone would want to harm him."

"No, he didn't." Miss Young's eyes narrowed. "Are you working for the police?"

"No, not at all. The truth is, they won't speak to us about the case, so we've been doing some investigating of our own. If we find out anything they need to know, we'll tell them, but so far we haven't."

"So you don't think it was me who poisoned Dr Shaw?"

"No, we don't and I'm sorry I upset you."

"That's a relief." Miss Young wiped her eyes with the back of a finger before picking up a small cream-filled tartlet. "I said earlier that Dr Shaw and I were old work colleagues, but if I'm being honest, I would have liked it to develop into something more. I certainly wouldn't have ended the relationship before it began."

Eliza smiled. "Did he have any idea?"

"I doubt it. As I said, when I saw him, he was too busy asking me about Brighton and where he should live."

"Which brings me back to my earlier question." Eliza dabbed her lips with a napkin. "Who in Brighton knew Dr Shaw well enough to want him dead?"


Once the cake stand was empty, Miss Young picked up her handbag and stood up. "Thank you for a lovely tea, but I'd better be getting home. Mother will be keen to hear all about the hotel."

"She's not been in, either?"

"No, and I doubt she ever will. She spends most of her days in bed."

"That's a shame." Eliza and Connie walked Miss Young to the foyer. "If we find out any more about Dr Shaw's death, we'll be in touch."

Once the doorman had opened the door for Miss Young, Eliza led the way to the table where the remnants of the men's afternoon tea were still obvious. Archie stood up when they joined them.

"How did you get on?"

Eliza slipped down on a chair. "Not as well as I'd hoped. She knew nothing about his plans, why he'd moved here or the letter."

"That's annoying."

"Or there's something she's not telling us."

"Oh ... if I may interrupt..." Sergeant Cooper grinned at them. "While you were busy, I spoke to the constable again, and he said they have about half a dozen samples of handwriting."

"Half a dozen. I wonder whose."

"I'm afraid he wouldn't say."

"I don't doubt it. We do know three, though. The two of us and Miss Young."

Mr Bell nodded. "They've probably asked the waitresses, too."

"Perhaps..." Eliza scrunched her nose as Connie interrupted.

"Miss Young did have one piece of news."

Eliza's eyes narrowed. "What was that?"

"That the police had tested the restaurant for arsenic and found nothing."

"Yes, of course, I'd almost forgotten. Not that I would have expected them to find anything."

Archie leaned forward, resting his elbows on his knees. "So she didn't add any arsenic to the glass of wine David drank?"

"It doesn't look like it." Eliza flinched as a gruff voice bellowed from behind them.

"What's going on here?"

Sergeant Cooper jumped to his feet. "Inspector Jarvis. It's not what you think…"

"Then what is it? I saw you with our constable this morning, no doubt finding out about the investigation, and now you're sitting with our key suspects."

"I'm sorry, sir, but you can't seriously believe any of these people would have murdered Dr Shaw. I've known them for years, and they wouldn't harm anyone."

"That's for me to determine, Sergeant. I very much hope the information we shared with you earlier was treated in confidence."

Sergeant Cooper stared at his feet before he looked directly at the inspector. "If you need any help with this investigation, sir, you could do worse than sharing your intelligence with Mrs Thomson and Mrs Appleton. They've been involved in a number of murder investigations over recent years and have helped the police immensely."

Inspector Jarvis snorted. "Nonsense."

"With all due respect, sir, it's no such thing. They can talk to people in a way we can't, especially other women. I'll be leaving Brighton shortly, but if I may offer you a piece of advice, don't discount the help these ladies can offer."

"I'll be the judge of whose help I need, Sergeant Cooper. Good day to you."

# CHAPTER FIFTEEN

Connie was in a dreamlike trance when Eliza met her by her bedroom door the following morning.

"Are you all right?"

"I'm fine, just reminiscing about yesterday. Frank and I had a lovely time together. It's a shame he had to leave so soon."

Eliza grinned at her. "I'm glad you enjoyed it; there'll be other chances to come together next year." She gestured for them to start walking.

"I hope so. I'm going to suggest we plan something as soon as I get home. Nothing more than a day trip, obviously."

"Obviously. It will give you something to look forward to, but could I have your attention for the rest of today?"

"Of course. What's the matter?"

"This business with David." The smile slipped from Eliza's face and she paused at the top of the stairs. "I've been awake for half the night thinking about it. The murder was clearly premeditated, but as hard as I try, I can't think of any reason why anyone in Brighton would want him dead."

Connie sighed. "Have you spoken to Dr Thomson about it?"

"Not since yesterday. He doesn't like being woken in the middle of the night."

Connie giggled. "I'm sure he doesn't. Why don't we ask him over breakfast?"

"I will. I just hope he's in a talkative mood."

Archie and Mr Bell were reading their newspapers when they arrived at the table and Archie was the first to fold his and place it on the table.

"Finally."

"I'm sorry. I didn't drop off to sleep until about five o'clock, so it took me a while to wake up."

Archie laughed as he pulled out a chair for her. "That's nothing new."

"It's not funny. I was thinking about David, and I can't work out why anyone down here would want him dead. Are you sure you've not forgotten to tell me anything?"

"Not that I can think of."

Mrs Dunn interrupted them as she came for their order. "Good morning. Will it be the four of you today, or are you expecting anyone else? You have a lot of visitors."

"Just the four of us today, thank you." Eliza glanced at the menu. "I'll have the same as usual. Scrambled eggs, please."

Once everyone else had placed their order, Eliza looked up at Archie. "Is there anyone from medical school who might live around here?"

"Not that I know of, but even if they did, I can't imagine why anyone would want to poison him. He was always very popular. I don't remember anyone who didn't like him."

"That doesn't surprise me." She leaned towards Connie.

"He used to be the life and soul of the party, surrounded by ladies. They loved his black hair and blue eyes."

"Might he have upset some of the gentlemen, then?"

Eliza raised her eyebrows at Archie. "What do you think?"

"I daresay he could have done, but it was a long time ago. Why wait until now to track him down?"

Mr Bell finally laid down his paper. "What about this woman he had dinner with on Saturday? Maybe she had a suitor who wasn't happy at seeing them together."

Eliza scrunched up her nose. "We didn't specifically ask about her situation, but she said she had designs on David herself. I doubt she'd say that if she was walking out with someone else."

Archie shrugged. "You may be surprised. He'd only just arrived, so she may have been testing the water, so to speak."

Eliza huffed as she spoke to Connie. "It looks like we'll need to speak to her again and ask if she has a gentleman friend."

"It would surprise me if she did. She seemed to spend most of her time caring for her mother."

"She did, but I still think we need to follow this up. Just in case. What if she wasn't seeing anyone, though? I'm at a loss at what to suggest."

Mr Bell's eyes narrowed. "Could the answer be in London? Your friend did seem rather pleased to be away from the place."

"You mean he may have been in trouble?" She grimaced at Archie. "Is that possible?"

"Who knows with David?"

Eliza looked at Connie. "I can feel a trip to the local library coming on."

"To check the newspapers?"

"Exactly." She turned to her father. "Will they have London newspapers here?"

"They should at least have *The Times.*"

"They will." Archie picked up his paper and waved it at her. "I've been reading it this morning, so it clearly makes its way this far."

"Good. If David was in any trouble, let's hope it was reported in the paper. What did he tell us when we met him, that he'd handed in his notice to leave St Thomas's a week before he left, and had finished work the day before he arrived at the hotel? It struck me at the time as being rather sudden."

Archie nodded. "Me too. It suggests that if he was trying to get away from someone or something, the problem probably only arose in the last month or so."

Connie raised an eyebrow. "Didn't he say something about his nerves, too?"

"Yes, he did." Eliza clapped her hands together. "I think we may have hit on something."

Archie shook his head. "Don't get carried away. You've a lot of newspapers to go through if you hope to find anything. Assuming it ended up in the newspaper."

Mr Bell squeezed his eyes shut. "Dr David Shaw and St Thomas's Hospital. I don't remember reading anything about either of them recently."

"Any news story would be easy to miss if you weren't looking for it."

"It would, but I'm usually good at recalling anything untoward. That must be where you get it from."

"Clearly." Eliza tittered. "If you don't mind, we'll visit the library, anyway."

"I wouldn't expect anything less." Mr Bell rubbed his hands together as his bacon and eggs arrived. "This should keep me going until luncheon."

The inside of the reference library was almost as grand as the Moorish-style exterior, although smaller than they were expecting. Eliza led the way to the front desk.

"Good morning. I wonder if you keep old copies of *The Times* here."

"We do, madam, but only back to 1895. Would you care to see them?"

"Please. We only need to look through the last few months."

They followed the short, squat man to a narrow flight of stairs that led to a mezzanine floor with books and periodicals to their left. "There they are. On the second shelf from the bottom. The dates are in chronological order and you can use the table here, to view them."

"Thank you." Eliza smiled as he left. "Now, where do we start? Perhaps a week last Friday when David handed in his notice of intent?"

They worked methodically through the newspapers, Connie scouring the left-hand page and Eliza the right. Eliza leaned in closer to page five of a newspaper from a week earlier. "What's this?"

Connie stopped and leaned across the table. "Something at St Thomas's?"

"Yes, here. St Thomas's Hospital, Lambeth has developed

a new type of surgery... Oh ... no. That won't have had anything to do with David..."

"Let's keep going, then."

They continued turning through the pages until they'd gone through the last six weeks of newspapers. As they turned the last one, Eliza straightened up. "Nothing."

"Have we gone back far enough?"

"I don't know, but even if we've not, there are no stories about doctors."

"Is that it, then?"

"It is for now." Eliza sighed as she returned the newspaper to the shelf. "It's almost time for coffee, but I suggest we pay Miss Young a visit instead."

"How will we find the house?"

"Archie gave me some money before we left, so we can take a carriage. It could be miles away."

"It had better not be. We'll miss luncheon too, if it is."

Eliza grinned. "Don't worry, I'll make sure we don't."

A row of carriages, with their horses impatiently kicking their front hooves, waited outside the small park opposite the library, and Eliza approached the one at the head of the queue.

"We need to go to an address on Freshfield Road. Could you tell us how close we are?"

"About a twenty-minute walk, longer if you're going to the top end."

"I'm not sure how far up we're going. Would you be able to take us?"

"It'll cost you sixpence."

"Oh, I've got money..."

The carriage driver nodded and got down from his seat to open the door. "Make yourselves comfortable."

The ride only took five minutes, and Eliza studied the weather-beaten front door as they waited for the driver to roll down the steps. She handed him a small silver coin.

"Would you wait for us? I don't expect we'll be long, and we need to get to the Metropole before luncheon. I've a shilling for you, if you do."

The man nodded. "That will get you twenty minutes."

"Thank you." Eliza hastened to the door with Connie behind her.

"I hope she's in after all this."

The smartly dressed woman of the previous afternoon had transformed into what looked like a housekeeper, with a faded navy dress covered with an apron. Hair hung loosely from the chignon that didn't appear to have been brushed since she'd got out of bed. She stepped backwards with a start when she opened the door.

"Mrs Thomson."

Eliza gave an apologetic smile. "I'm sorry to trouble you unannounced, but we realised there were one or two questions we'd forgotten to ask. May we come in?"

When Miss Young hesitated, Eliza gestured to the carriage. "We won't keep you. The driver will only wait for twenty minutes..."

"Very well." She pulled open the door and showed them into the neatly arranged front room. "We can talk in here. Please, take a seat." She indicated to two dark green armchairs on either side of the fireplace. "What would you like to know?"

Eliza cleared her throat. "I hope you don't think we're prying, but are you walking out with anyone?"

Her eyes narrowed. "Me? No. Why?"

"Is there anyone you've been close to while you've been in Brighton?"

"No. I told you, I've been busy looking after Mother. I've no time for frivolities."

"And yet you suggested you'd like a relationship with Dr Shaw?"

She sighed. "That would have been different."

"How?"

"Because he'd have been worth it ... and he wouldn't have had too many expectations of me. Most men of my age are widows and only want a wife to act as a housekeeper or mother to their children. I don't need anyone else to look after. Why do you ask?"

"We wondered if there was someone in your life who may have been jealous seeing you with Dr Shaw."

"Ah, I see. No, I can assure you, no one is that interested in me. Except Mother, of course, but given she isn't able to get out of bed unaided, I wouldn't worry about her."

"I don't suppose it's a nice reason for an alibi, but it's helpful, thank you. Another line of thought was that Dr Shaw's death may somehow be connected to events in London."

"London?" Miss Young's mouth fell open as her gaze shifted between them. "How?"

"That's what we were hoping you could help with. Dr Shaw seemed to leave St Thomas's rather quickly, and we wondered if you knew why."

"N-no. Why would I?" Her eyes flicked between them. "I've been down here for over six months."

"But while you worked with Dr Shaw, were you aware of him falling out with anyone, or even having any disagreements?"

"No, not at all. He was popular with everyone on the ward."

"What about the patients?"

Her brow creased. "They were all children…"

"Ah, yes. What about their parents, then?"

Miss Young shrugged. "He didn't have much to do with them, that was left to us…"

"So there were no scandals?"

"What do you mean?"

"I don't know. Did he break anyone's heart, perhaps?"

Miss Young stared at the floor. "I doubt he'd have told me if he had."

"No, you're right. I'm sorry." Eliza stood up. "We'd better go. Thank you for your time. If you happen to think of any reason, however slight, why anyone would want to harm him, would you contact us at the hotel?"

Miss Young ushered them to the door. "I will, although I doubt I'll be able to help."

# CHAPTER SIXTEEN

Colonel and Mrs Giles were sitting at a table with Mr and Mrs Brooks when Archie led their party into the lounge after luncheon. Mr Brooks beckoned them over.

"Will you join us? We've been wondering how you're getting along with your investigations."

Eliza accepted the chair the colonel pulled out for her. "Thank you, although I'm not sure we'll be able to satisfy your curiosity." She paused as Mrs Dunn joined them.

"Is it tea for four?"

"Yes, please." Archie took the seat opposite his wife and once Mrs Dunn had left, Mr Brooks leaned over to them.

"Do you know if the police are any closer to an answer than you are?"

Eliza sighed. "I'm afraid we can't say. We heard yesterday that they'd found traces of arsenic on the bar, but they hadn't found where it had come from. We don't believe they've worked out a motive, either."

"And do you have any ideas?"

"None. It's so bizarre. We knew Dr Shaw, but for the life

of us, we can't fathom why anyone would want him dead. Let alone anyone in Brighton, given he'd been here for less than twelve hours when he was poisoned."

"Yes ... that is curious." The colonel ran a finger over his moustache. "I'd suggest it was someone in the hotel who poisoned him."

"What makes you say that?"

"Oh, I've no evidence, but when I was in the army, if there were ever any disagreements amongst the men, it was usually amongst those in the same dormitories."

"But the hotel houses hundreds of people." Eliza studied those close by. "Not only that, many of the people here aren't even residents. People will often just come in for a drink or something to eat. It's like trying to find a needle in a haystack."

The colonel studied the tables nearby. "Have you spoken to the staff who were working on Saturday?"

Eliza nodded. "All who came into contact with him."

"And you've found nothing?"

She shook her head. "Nobody has admitted to knowing him before Saturday."

Mr Brooks lowered his voice. "Could they be lying?"

Eliza glanced at Connie and then at Archie. "I suppose so, but if they were, they were very good at it."

The colonel looked Eliza in the eye. "Ask them again. See if their stories stay the same. It's usually a good indication..."

Mrs Dunn appeared with a tray and placed it on the table. "Your tea, sir, and a selection of petits fours. Will there be anything else?"

The colonel stood up to address her. "A question, if I may, young lady. We wondered if the police have spoken to all the staff about the incident at the weekend, yet."

"Oh ... I really can't say, sir. They've spoken to a lot of us..."

"And when you talk amongst yourselves, are you aware of anyone who may have been acquainted with Dr Shaw before he came to Brighton?"

Mrs Dunn glanced around eight pairs of expectant eyes. "N-no ... we've not been talking about it. We've been told not to."

Eliza cocked her head to one side. "Who by?"

"Our bosses..."

"Not the police?"

"T-they've not said much at all. They asked if we'd had anything to do with the gentleman in question, if we'd come across him before he got to the Metropole and if we had access to any rat poison."

"And that was it?"

"That was all they asked me and my husband, so I suppose that's all they asked everyone else."

"You and your husband both helped Dr Shaw when he got here. Didn't they want to know any more about that?"

"Oh, yes, but they only wanted to check what he'd said to us, which wasn't much. He asked me for a spare cup and saucer, and my husband took his bags upstairs. That was what we told them."

"Did they ask for a sample of your handwriting, by any chance?"

"Why would they do that?"

"We heard there was a letter in Dr Shaw's room, but nobody knows who wrote it."

Mrs Dunn looked around to see a guest signalling to her. "I'm sorry. I need to go."

"Very well, thank you..." Eliza's smile disappeared as Mrs Dunn hurried away. "She looked pleased to leave. It's strange they didn't ask to see her handwriting."

Archie grunted. "Given she only saw him briefly and didn't serve him any drinks, I suspect they didn't think they needed to."

"Well, they should have done." Eliza let out a deep sigh. "If you want my opinion, the police are completely out of their depth."

"Don't be too harsh. I don't suppose they get many murders around here."

Colonel Giles stroked his moustache. "Whether they do or not, I'd still wager that the culprit is within these walls. You just need to find them."

The promenade was busy as Eliza and Connie strolled behind Archie and Mr Bell towards the pier.

Connie sniffed the sea air. "It would be so relaxing if it wasn't for this investigation."

"It would..."

"Would you say the colonel has a point? About the killer being in the same hotel."

"Probably. I can't think how anyone else would know David was here unless they followed him, but if that were the case, I'm sure someone would have seen them skulking around the foyer."

"They may have done, but we've not directly asked anyone."

"No." Eliza stared out across the sea. "We should ask Mr Topham, to be on the safe side, but it may well be someone closer to the hotel. I'm sure we're missing something."

"Is that why you're not saying much?"

"There's something niggling me. Oh!" Her eyes widened as she grabbed Connie's arms. "That's it!"

"What is?"

"Do you remember when we were in the library? There was a story about St Thomas's Hospital."

"Something about a new surgical technique?" Connie's forehead creased. "You said it wasn't important."

"And it wasn't, but something about it has just occurred to me. Lambeth!"

"Lambeth?"

"Yes! The newspaper reminded me that St Thomas's is in Lambeth, and I've just realised it's the second time this week I've come across it."

Connie's eyes narrowed. "When else have you heard it?"

"Do you remember on Saturday, shortly after we arrived, we went for afternoon tea?"

"What of it?"

"Mrs Dunn was very chatty and asked where we'd travelled from. When we were talking, she said that before moving to Brighton, her and her husband had lived in London. Or to be more specific, Lambeth."

Connie gasped. "You're right. Are you suggesting they knew Dr Shaw?"

"I've no idea, but it's quite a coincidence."

"Will you ask them?"

Eliza's shoulders drooped. "I'm not sure there's much point at the moment. We've already asked them if they knew David. In fact, we've asked Mrs Dunn twice, and they've both denied ever seeing him before. If we speak to them again, we need some reason to believe they're lying."

"How do we find out?"

Eliza huffed. "I don't know."

Archie and Mr Bell were waiting at the entrance to the pier when they joined them, and Archie extended an arm to usher them to the right.

"What have you been doing? We could be at the other end of the pier by now."

"I'm sorry. I've been thinking."

"Can't you do the two things at once?"

Eliza raised an eyebrow at him. "Normally, I can, but I had a particularly important thought and I needed to work it through."

Mr Bell walked beside Connie as they set off along the pier, their shoes clicking on the wooden boards that stretched out over the sea. He looked over to Eliza. "Are you going to tell us about it?"

"It's still only an idea, but in a nutshell, it's possible that the Dunns knew David in London."

Archie stared at her. "How? They told us they didn't."

"And they may not have, but it suddenly dawned on me that they all lived in Lambeth before they moved here."

"Lambeth's a big place. And the Dunns have been down here for months."

"Since the start of the season, Mrs Dunn said. Still, it's quite a coincidence, don't you think?"

"Well, yes, but if they disliked David enough to want him dead, it seems strange that he would move closer to them."

"He may not have known they were here."

"In which case, he's unlikely to have told them he was

coming, so why would they poison him on the first afternoon?"

"That's what I need to work out." Eliza stared out to sea as Archie patted her hand.

"You know as well as I do it was turned four when David arrived at the hotel on Saturday, and he'd most likely been poisoned by the time he left for dinner at half past six. Mrs Dunn was serving afternoon tea when we first saw him, and her husband was looking after his bags and helping other guests. Even if they'd wanted to murder him, they'd have had no opportunity to buy any poison before the shops closed at five."

Mr Bell nodded. "And it's hardly the sort of thing you'd carry around on the off-chance."

Eliza bit her lip as she carried on walking. "That might make sense, but the fact of the matter is that somebody did poison him … apparently at short notice."

"But where did they get the arsenic from?" Mr Bell shook his head. "The police have been to all the local stores, and nobody from the hotel had bought any in the last month, let alone on Saturday."

"You're right, again, but–" a smile returned to her lips "– what if they didn't need to go out for it? What if the killer had access to the hotel supplies? They could have used that. There's a good chance it's not even the dyed variety."

Connie grinned at her. "We never found out which version of the arsenic the police found. Knowing what's in the hotel might help."

"Yes!" She beamed at Archie. "We have to speak to the inspector when we get back to the hotel, assuming he's still there, and find out what they know. We also need to find out who has access to the supply room."

"Very well, but let me do the talking. You know he's uncomfortable sharing information with you."

"Only because he knows I'm right."

"That's as maybe, but I suggest we take a more passive approach and see what he'll tell us."

# CHAPTER SEVENTEEN

There was no sign of either Mr Topham or the police when they returned to the hotel, and Archie ushered them all into the lounge towards the table by the window. He pulled out Eliza's usual chair with a view of the sea, but she declined.

"Do you mind if I sit facing the room so I can watch what's going on?"

"What are you hoping to see?"

"The police, for one thing. I wondered if the Brookses or Gileses would be around, too, but they must still be out."

Connie accepted the seat beside her. "I wonder what happened to the ladies who sat with us the other day. They were very interested in what was going on, but we've not seen them since. I didn't think they were due to go home until Saturday."

"No, me neither. They're probably playing bridge again."

"Making the most of being down here." Connie chuckled. "If the Brookses or Gileses join us, will we tell them about Lambeth?"

Eliza looked at Archie. "I'm not sure. What do you say?"

"We should keep it to ourselves for now. It's nothing more than an idea at the moment."

Miss Anderson interrupted as she stood beside Archie, her pencil poised over her notebook. "Good afternoon, all. What may I get you?"

Eliza glanced around the room before staring up at her. "No Mrs Dunn today?"

"It's her day off, so she's gone out with her mother."

*Convenient.* "Does she always take Wednesdays off?"

"Unless there's a reason not to."

"Does Mr Dunn do the same?"

"Not usually. He's always looking for overtime, so he'll work seven days a week if he can."

"He must be exhausted."

Miss Anderson shrugged. "The money focuses his mind. Now, would you like afternoon tea?"

Archie shook his head. "Just a pot of tea and a plate of biscuits, please. We don't seem to manage dinner if we eat sandwiches and cakes at this time."

Miss Anderson grinned. "I quite understand. I'm sure I wouldn't, either." As she left, Eliza sat back with her eyes on the archway into the foyer.

"It's typical the police aren't here this afternoon. Might they be in the bar?"

Mr Bell pushed himself up. "Shall I check?"

"If you don't mind."

Archie joined Mr Bell on his feet. "I'll go with him in case they are. They may talk to me more than you."

Eliza grinned. "A likely tale. I think it's just another excuse for a snifter."

"As if... We won't be long."

Eliza waited for them to leave before turning to peer over her shoulder towards the window. "I can see I'm going to have another sleepless night wondering how the Dunns might have known David. They've not shown a hint of recognition..."

"Could you ask the police when you speak to them about the arsenic?"

Eliza stared at her. "The police? I doubt they'll even know about it."

"Oh, I didn't mean that. I was thinking that they'll probably know people in London who could check if there was any way the Dunns could come into contact with Dr Shaw. Perhaps they lived near each other ... or the Dunns may have visited the hospital..."

Eliza's face lit up. "That could be it! Connie, you're a genius. We need to make a list of questions for when we see them. Let me get my notebook..." She rummaged in her bag for several seconds before she pulled it out and set her bag back on the floor. "Here we are. Now..."

"Mrs Thomson."

Eliza's head shot up and she let out a low groan. "He doesn't sound happy."

The inspector was still halfway across the room and she waited until he joined them. "Inspector Jarvis. My husband found you, I see."

"And I'm grateful he did. I told you in no uncertain terms last Sunday to stay away from our investigation."

She forced a smile. "Forgive me. I didn't realise I had anything to do with it. Are you making good progress?"

"We've had a breakthrough today, as it happens."

"Really! What sort of breakthrough?"

"That, madam, is of no concern to you."

Her shoulders dropped. "That's a matter of opinion. Dr Shaw was an old friend of ours, yet you accused me and my husband of being involved in his death. If you're ready to arrest someone else, it would be nice to know."

"It wasn't that sort of breakthrough."

Eliza's eyes narrowed. "I'm sorry, Inspector, but what exactly do you expect us to do? Despite being suspects, you've given us no information for days, so you can hardly blame us for trying to help ourselves."

"We've had several members of staff not wanting to talk to us, because they've already told you all they know."

"I thought you'd spoken to everyone before we did."

"That is not the point, Mrs Thomson. You are *contaminating* our witnesses with your gossip, and I won't tolerate it."

"I'll try to be more discreet in future."

Inspector Jarvis turned to Archie, who had joined them. "That is not what I meant. I don't want her meddling in the case any longer. Is that understood?"

Eliza's face burned as Inspector Jarvis stormed out into the foyer, and she stared at Archie as he took the seat opposite her. "What on earth did you say to him?"

"Nothing."

She looked at her father. "What did he say?"

"There were several police in the bar testing the floor, and all we did was ask if they'd found where the arsenic had come from."

"It's true." Archie exchanged a glance with his father-in-law. "The constable was helpful and told us that they'd found traces of poison around the edges of most of the reception rooms. The problem is, it's white arsenic, so they've no idea where it's come from. I told him you'd been talking about white arsenic, but I said your name just as Jarvis arrived and he got rather irate. You saw what happened next."

"That was all because I'd been thinking about the poison! I'll show him. He hasn't got a clue what he's doing, and after that outburst, I won't be helping him." She turned to Connie. "I'll write to Inspector Adams instead."

"What? Wait a minute..." Archie's mouth opened and closed without any words coming out. "Why are you bringing Inspector Adams into this?"

"I wasn't going to, but Inspector Jarvis has forced me into it. Connie had an idea, and I was going to ask Inspector Jarvis for help, but he can forget it now."

"What idea?"

Eliza paused as Miss Anderson returned with their tea.

"Here we are. I'm sorry for the delay. The police have been asking questions again."

Eliza raised an eyebrow. "What did they want to know?"

"Only if the hotel has its own supply of rat poison, which, of course, it does. They've gone off to speak to the manager about it."

"Do all the staff have access to it?"

Miss Anderson frowned. "Not all of us. I don't even know where it is. I couldn't tell you who does, either. If the serving staff ever has need for it, we call the maintenance men. They put it out every month or so, but if anyone suspects rats in the meantime, they ask them to sort it out."

"Who are these men? Do we know them?"

"I doubt it. They tend to work behind the scenes, and don't usually work at weekends unless there's a problem. If you're wondering if they could have poisoned Dr Shaw, I'm afraid the answer is no. They weren't here."

"All right, thank you." Eliza watched Miss Anderson leave. "If they put arsenic all around the hotel, could someone have swept it up and put it into David's drink?"

Archie stood up. "Let's have a look, shall we?" He peered behind Eliza's chair. "There's nothing obvious there, so either they haven't been very thorough or it's in small amounts."

"Not enough to make a man ill?"

"Not unless they swept the whole hotel. Or had access to the store."

Eliza turned back to the table and picked up the milk jug. "It must be someone who could get into the store, which would limit the list of suspects. It shouldn't be difficult to find out who."

Mr Bell watched Connie as she poured the tea. "What about the porters?"

"Mr Dunn. Yes!" Eliza gasped at Archie. "Any of the men who work in the foyer must know where the key's kept. Assuming the room is locked. It would be easy for one of them to take it."

He nodded. "You're probably right."

"Thankfully, Inspector Jarvis won't be here all evening, so you'll be able to ask a few questions while you're in the bar later. In the meantime, I'll write to Inspector Adams."

Archie checked his pocket watch. "You've left it a bit late. The last post will be going shortly, and even if you make it, you won't get a reply from him until Friday at the earliest."

"You're right. We'll need to send a telegram."

"That's not what I meant…"

Eliza shook her head. "Don't look so worried. I'll cut down on the number of words I need…"

"I don't know how. You can't ask a string of questions when you're paying by the word … and we're not made of money."

"It will be worth it if we can find a link to the Dunns." She smiled at her father. "Please."

Mr Bell rolled his eyes. "Very well. But keep it brief. I draw the line at half-a-crown."

Eliza grinned at him. "Thank you. I'll work on it now so you can check it."

# CHAPTER EIGHTEEN

M r and Mrs Brooks were at their usual table when Eliza and Connie strolled into the lounge following dinner.

"Do you mind if we join you?"

"Not at all. We'd be disappointed if you didn't." Mr Brooks stood up to help them into their chairs. "I spoke to the colonel earlier and he and Mrs Giles will join us presently, too. Are your gentlemen in the bar?"

"They are. They seem to have made rather a habit of it. Not that they'll stay long. Have you had a nice day?"

"Yes, very. We walked up to Queen's Park this morning, which was delightful. Once we'd had luncheon, we decided we'd done enough walking for one day, so we sat on the beach for a couple of hours this afternoon."

Eliza grimaced. "Please don't tell my husband. He has an idea that we should do that, but this investigation has put us all off."

"Then may I suggest you have a rethink." Mrs Brooks sat

up straight. "We had a lovely time, especially watching those brave souls go into the water. It was rather amusing seeing them jump backwards because of the cold."

"Which is one reason I won't be going in." Eliza looked up as Mrs Giles arrived beside her. "Good evening. Are you on your own?"

"I am, but I won't be for long. My husband saw you were here and decided Dr Thomson must be in the bar. I hope you don't mind me joining you."

"Not at all." Mr Brooks pulled up a chair for her. "We were telling Mrs Thomson and Mrs Appleton about our afternoon on the beach. Have you ventured down there yet?"

"Gracious, no. You won't get my husband sitting in one of those deckchairs. We prefer to walk along the promenade towards the next town and take a seat when we get there before walking back. It's rather pleasant."

"We've done that ourselves... Ah, here's Miss Anderson."

The waitress put down a tray of tea and petits fours for the Brookses before she turned to the ladies. "Would you care for the same?"

Eliza nodded. "Please, but only for the three of us. Our husbands can order later if they want anything."

"Very good, madam."

Mr Brooks leaned towards Eliza. "Do you have any more news for us today?"

Eliza sighed. "Not a lot, but we've learned that the police found more rat poison in the bar area and that it was white arsenic."

"So the killer wouldn't have bought it from a shop."

"That's what it looks like." Eliza studied Mr Brooks.

"We've a theory that the poison could be from the hotel's own stores. Might you have any idea where that would be, or what else might be stored with it?"

He scanned the faces of the ladies surrounding him. "Not really, but I imagine it would be in the basement, perhaps near the kitchen, where rats would search for food."

"That makes sense. Would they lock it away?"

He puffed out his cheeks. "I daresay it should be in this day and age, especially in a hotel like this, but you can never discount someone leaving a door open."

"You're right." Eliza's eyes narrowed. "Miss Anderson told us earlier that there are maintenance men who deal with the vermin, but that they don't work at weekends. I wonder if they'd leave the door open, or pass someone the key, so they didn't need to come in on their days off."

"Mr Dunn." Connie spoke to no one in particular, but flinched when Eliza stared at her. "Don't look at me like that. Miss Anderson said he was always happy to do overtime. What if he helped the maintenance men out with a bit of rat-catching?"

"You're right! Connie, not for the first time today, you're a genius!"

Mr Brooks's mouth fell open. "You think the porter did it?"

"Oh, no ... not at the moment. We're just keeping an eye on him."

"But why? The last I heard, all he'd done was help Dr Shaw with his bags."

"That's why we can't pin anything on him, but I can't help thinking the colonel was right when he said the killer was likely to be in the hotel, and Mr Dunn was one of the few people to come into contact with him."

"But there are hundreds of other people staying here."

Eliza's shoulders sagged. "I know. The theory needs more work yet." She turned as footsteps approached behind her. "Good evening, Colonel. That was quick. Haven't you brought my husband and father with you?"

"They're on their way." He took the seat beside his wife. "They've been telling me about the investigation, but it seems that no one's any the wiser about the killer. It's dashed confusing."

"It certainly is. Have you had any further thoughts?"

"None, I'm afraid. I had a word with the doorman earlier, though. Wanted to check whether he'd seen anyone acting suspiciously."

"And had he?"

"No. Not a soul."

"Oh."

The colonel smiled at her. "There's no need to be downcast. I'd say it confirms my suspicion that the perpetrator is part of the setup. That way, nobody would notice them."

"A member of staff, perhaps..." Eliza raised an eyebrow.

"It could well be..." The colonel stood up as Mrs Gardener and Mrs Smith arrived. "Good evening, ladies. Will you join us?"

"That would be lovely." Mrs Smith sighed as she accepted the chair the colonel held out for her. "We've had a pleasant time with our friend, but we feel as if we've missed out here. What's the latest news?"

Eliza creased her cheek. "We've not much to report, but I don't remember where we were up to when we last spoke."

"We told you we'd seen Dr Shaw looking rather drunk, and you suggested we tell the police."

"Oh, yes. Did you?"

"We did. Not that they had much to say. All they did was take a note of it and we've not heard from them since."

Eliza twisted her lip. "They seem to be preoccupied with the poison, almost to the exclusion of everything else. I'm afraid that other than hearing it was white arsenic, we're not much further on. The biggest problem is that we can't find anyone with a motive for wanting Dr Shaw dead."

Mrs Gardener adjusted her pince-nez as she studied her. "No motive? There must be."

"Well ... yes, but we've no idea what it is. Dr Shaw had only been in Brighton for three hours at the most before the first dose of poison was administered. How could anyone even know he was here?"

"How strange." Mrs Gardener looked at her sister-in-law. "I don't know whether this will help, but do you remember there was a man talking to a porter when we arrived back here on Saturday evening? I didn't give him a second glance at the time, but I've been thinking about it, and he did look rather suspicious."

"A man acting suspiciously?" Eliza's eyes darted towards Connie but Mrs Smith ignored her.

"You mean that stocky man?"

"Yes."

"Well, I couldn't say. As you know, I didn't pay much attention after Dr Shaw nearly knocked me over, but I thought I heard men's voices as we went inside... I presumed it was him and the porter..."

Eliza sat forward on the edge of her seat. "Forgive me for

interrupting, but who was this man? And who was the porter? Would they have seen Dr Shaw?"

Mrs Gardener nodded. "They'd almost certainly have noticed him when he rushed past. I hadn't seen the stocky man before, but they were standing on the far side of the portico when we arrived. The man in question had his back to us, but Mr Dunn, the porter, acknowledged us as we turned into the hotel."

"Mr Dunn! And this was around midnight?"

"Yes. When we got back from playing bridge."

Eliza stared at Connie. "He told us he'd left the hotel at eleven o'clock. Why would he do that?"

"Perhaps he had, but then he came back."

"Then why not tell us?" Eliza edged closer to Mrs Gardener. "Can you tell us anything else about the man he was with? His height, the colour of his hair...?"

"Let me think." Her forehead creased. "If I remember rightly, he was slightly shorter than Mr Dunn, and there was hair protruding from the rim of his summer hat. The night was dark so I can't say much more."

"What was he wearing?"

"A dark jacket with light trousers. As I say, I didn't see his face, so I can't be more specific."

"That's still helpful. Thank you. Do you think he was staying at the hotel?"

"I really couldn't say. We dashed in without a backward glance."

"Yes, you said." Eliza looked back at Connie. "We'll need to speak to Mr Dunn again. He may be able to help us." She flinched as a hand touched her shoulder, but returned Archie's smile as he gazed down at her.

"What are you speaking to Mr Dunn about now?"

"Mrs Gardener remembered he was outside with a stranger when David left the hotel. We need to know why he didn't tell us. And find out who the other man was."

Archie checked his pocket watch. "A job for tomorrow, I'd say. It's almost time for bed."

# CHAPTER NINETEEN

The sun filled the right-hand side of the dining room the following morning, and the curtains had already been pulled across the windows when Eliza and Connie arrived at their table.

"It's such a shame to block out the daylight, but I suppose it can't be helped."

"It's better than being blinded." Archie held out Eliza's now familiar chair.

"It is. Right, what do I want this morning? I'm not that hungry."

Mr Bell tucked his napkin into his collar. "I'm going to try the kedgeree. I saw someone with it yesterday and it looked rather nice."

"It did, I noticed that. It would be too much for me, though..." She paused as a waitress joined them. "Good morning. Just a bowl of breakfast cereal and a round of toast for me, please."

"Very good, madam." She worked around the table, taking the other orders, but as she left, a bellboy joined them.

"Good morning, Dr Thomson." He bowed and offered Archie an envelope. "This has arrived for Mrs Thomson."

Archie raised an eyebrow as he took the correspondence. "That was quick. Thank you." He pressed a penny into the boy's hand and waited for him to leave before he passed it across the table to Eliza. "Inspector Adams, I presume."

"A telegram, too. I hope that means he's found something." The flap of the envelope was already open and Eliza pulled out a single sheet of paper and held it between her and Connie.

*Dr Shaw patient died Dec 5 1903 STOP Aged two STOP Name Thomas Dunn STOP Insp Adams*

Eliza's mouth fell open as she read, and she passed the letter to Archie. "Our motive."

"Good grief." Archie shared the telegram with Mr Bell as Eliza took a deep breath.

"That can't be a coincidence."

Archie passed the paper back to her. "When did the Dunns come to Brighton? Was it March?"

"That's what they said."

"So about three months after the child's death."

Connie's eyes narrowed. "Could the timing cast a doubt on the child being theirs? They should be in mourning, but there's not much sign of it."

"Mrs Dunn's black-and-white uniform is probably enough in this day and age."

"That's true. Things are a lot less obvious than they used to be."

Eliza looked at Archie. "If they *are* the parents, do you think David came to Brighton looking for them?"

He shrugged. "Somehow I doubt it, but it might be the reason he left the hospital in such a hurry. If they'd held an enquiry..."

"It would have taken that long for them to reach a conclusion, especially with Christmas in the way. Perhaps he was about to lose his job, so he left before they got the chance to serve him notice."

"That sounds like the sort of thing David would do. Run away and pretend that nothing happened."

"So you don't think he came here deliberately?"

"Who knows? As you say, casually bumping into the Dunns is rather a coincidence." Archie blew out his cheeks as Mr Bell turned to him.

"Maybe he wanted to get them to drop the charges, assuming they were the ones who raised the complaint."

"That would make more sense, although based on the timings he wouldn't have had chance to speak to them. He was either with us or having dinner with his young lady."

"Hmm." Mr Bell rubbed his cheek. "There was a short period while we were dressing for dinner..."

Connie drummed her fingers on the table. "Didn't he change for dinner himself? I'm almost sure he wore a different jacket when he went out."

"If he did, he definitely wouldn't have had time to talk to them, which means they may not have known why he was here."

Eliza sighed. "We need to check."

Archie banged the table. "Why didn't David mention it to me? We spent over an hour together on Saturday evening when he came back from the restaurant. I could have helped before things got out of hand."

"He wouldn't have known he was so short of time. It's frustrating he had to go out on Saturday evening. He'd have had dinner with us otherwise."

Connie looked over to Eliza. "Do you think he'd have said anything to Miss Young?"

"Of course!" Eliza beamed at her. "I always had a feeling she was hiding something. I wonder if this is it." She sat back as the waitress arrived with breakfast. "I'm glad I didn't ask for much, I'm far too busy to worry about eating." She glanced at Connie's plate of scrambled eggs. "We should visit Miss Young first and hope she can confirm the link between the Dunns and the child. Then we'll speak to Mr and Mrs Dunn."

Miss Young took a step backwards as she opened the door to Eliza and Connie. "Oh ... I wasn't expecting you."

Eliza found her most gracious smile. "We're sorry to disturb you again, but some information has come to light, and we'd like to ask you about it. Do you mind if we come in?"

"Er ... no. This way." She showed them into the front room. "How may I help?"

"We believe there was an issue at St Thomas's at the end of last year where a child died."

Miss Young's face paled, and she wandered to the window, keeping her back to the room. "I knew nothing of it. I'd long since moved to another ward and then I moved down here..."

"But you were aware that David was in trouble? Is that why you suggested he move to Brighton?"

Miss Young's shoulders rose and fell. "He was going to lose his livelihood. I had to do something."

"How did you find out about it?" Eliza glanced at Connie when Miss Young failed to answer. "Miss Young?"

Her gentle sobs gradually grew louder. "I wasn't strictly honest with you the other day. It's true that I left David's ward a couple of years ago, but we kept in touch. I'd often invite him to the house for dinner... He was on his own, you see, and it didn't seem right that he should cook for himself..."

"Was there any more to it than having dinner?"

She shook her head. "I'd hoped there might be, but he was always so busy..."

"So when you moved down here to be with your mother, you devised a plan to bring him here, too."

"No, not at all. I had a duty down here and I originally planned to return to London when Mother no longer needed me..."

"But then you heard about the incident?"

She nodded. "I was only trying to help."

"But you must have thought that if you were the only person he knew down here, it would bring you closer together?"

She wiped her eyes with the back of a hand. "I'd suggested it several times, but he'd laughed it off until the enquiry found him guilty. He suddenly liked the idea of moving, and it helped that I'd be here to help him settle in."

"Why didn't you tell us?"

She shrugged. "He didn't want anyone knowing about it."

"Even after his death?"

"I didn't want to sully his reputation."

"Well, it may have been helpful, because there's a

possibility the issue in London was directly responsible for his murder. Did you ever meet the parents of the child who died?"

"No."

Her response was a bit too quick and Eliza bit her lip. "I'm afraid I'm struggling to believe you. Are you sure you didn't see one or other of the parents in the hotel on Tuesday when you joined us for afternoon tea?"

"No!" Miss Young spun round. "How could I when I'd never met them?"

"You're sure?"

"I promise. I know they reported David to the hospital manager, and that they didn't want him working with children any more, but that was it. He didn't even tell me their names."

"Have you heard the name Thomas Dunn?"

Miss Young momentarily froze. "I have, but I didn't know who he was. When David told me what was going on, he just referred to him as 'the child'. He never gave a name. I must have heard it from someone else in the hospital."

"So you couldn't identify the parents if you saw them?"

"No." She stared at Eliza. "If the parents are in the hotel, are you suggesting they were the ones who killed David?"

"It's a possibility."

"And you think I'm protecting them? How could I when they've taken from me the one man I'd hoped to settle down with? If I saw them, I'd..."

Eliza held up a hand. "Please, don't upset yourself. One of the reasons I asked if you knew them is because we need to be sure that the Mr and Mrs Dunn working in the Metropole are actually the parents of young Thomas. It's not such an uncommon name that we may be mistaken."

"Can't you just ask them?"

"We can, but their record of telling the truth is worse than yours. They've both denied ever seeing David before Saturday."

Miss Young wiped her eyes on her handkerchief. "I wish I could help, then. If they were responsible for David's death, I'd like to see them go to the gallows."

# CHAPTER TWENTY

The jostling of the carriage along the cobbled streets as they travelled back to the hotel made it difficult for Eliza to write up her thoughts. She pushed her notebook into her bag with a sigh.

"That will have to do. Thankfully, I only wrote it in pencil, so I can tidy it up later." She peered through the window as the carriage came to a stop. "We could do with Mr Dunn being in work. I don't want to wait too long to speak to him."

"Mrs Dunn should be around, even if he's not."

"I hope so." She accepted the coachman's hand as he helped her down the carriage steps, and Mr Topham raised his hat as he held open the door for them.

"Welcome back, ladies. Have you had a pleasant morning?"

"Productive, thank you. Can you tell us if Mr Dunn's working today?"

"He'll be in at three, madam."

"Very good." She turned to Connie. "Let's find Mrs Dunn instead."

They strolled into the lounge and Eliza glanced around their usual tables. "It's quiet in here."

"No sign of Dr Thomson or Mr Bell, even."

She grinned. "It wouldn't surprise me if they've gone to the beach. After Mrs Brooks's recommendation yesterday, I suggested they go."

"While we were out of the way."

Eliza laughed. "Exactly." She gazed over at the clock. "It's turned eleven, so we don't need to wait for them for coffee. It's not our fault they're late."

They took their seat in the window, and Connie nudged Eliza as Mrs Dunn appeared. "We're in luck. Will you question her now?"

"Shall we get our coffee first? She may not want to serve us once we've spoken to her."

Connie grimaced. "I hadn't thought of that."

Mrs Dunn smiled as she arrived at their table. "Is it just the two of you today?"

"It is. I couldn't tell you where my husband is."

"Would you like me to bring another two cups in case they arrive?"

Eliza looked at Connie. "Erm ... no, thank you. If they leave it much longer, it will be too late. Thank you, anyway." She watched as Mrs Dunn left them. "I can't decide how to approach her when she gets back. I can't be harsh if she's recently bereaved."

"Don't you need to check it was her son first?"

"Yes, I do. It's all rather delicate, though..." Her voice trailed off as Archie and Mr Bell strode into the lounge and headed straight towards them. "Typical of them to arrive now."

"What's the matter? You don't look very pleased to see us."

"It's not that. You've just picked the wrong time. Mrs Dunn's gone for our coffee, and I want to talk to her when she comes back. Would you mind waiting outside for ten minutes?"

Archie raised an eyebrow at Mr Bell. "We can do better than that. Shall we take elevenses in the bar?"

"What a splendid idea." He grinned at Eliza. "Half an hour should give you plenty of time."

"And no more!" A suppressed grin offset her stern voice. "It would be nice to take a walk before luncheon once we've finished here."

Archie and Mr Bell had only just disappeared when Mrs Dunn returned with their tray.

"Here we are."

Eliza watched her place the cups and saucers onto the table. "The lounge is quiet this morning."

"It is. People prefer to go out early before the sun gets too high."

"I don't blame them." Eliza forced a smile. "I wonder if now might be a good time to ask you a few questions. About Dr Shaw."

Mrs Dunn's eyes shifted around the room. "What sort of questions?"

"They are rather delicate, I'm afraid." Eliza pursed her lips. "Am I right in thinking you moved down to Brighton in March of this year?"

"Yes, the nineteenth, so we had time for some training before the start of the season at Easter."

"Can you remind me why you moved to Brighton?"

"We ... erm ... we wanted to get away from London. All that smog..."

"It is dreadful, but I wonder if that's the real reason." Eliza took a deep breath. "I'm sorry to have to ask you this, but had you suffered a bereavement before you moved here? At the end of 1903?"

Mrs Dunn's eyes were the only things that moved as they flicked between Eliza and Connie. "W-who told you that?"

"So it's true?"

"What's true?"

"I don't like to bring this up while you're working, but we understand a young boy called Thomas Dunn passed away in December last year at St Thomas's hospital in Lambeth. Was he your son?"

Eliza paused but Mrs Dunn remained silent.

"We'll be able to confirm the parents' identity when we get back to London, but it would be easier if you could help us while we're here."

"Do the police know?"

"Not the local police ... or at least, not as far as we're aware."

Mrs Dunn's eyes continued to flicker between them. "Then how did you find out?"

"We've a connection in London. We've also heard that the doctor responsible for the child was Dr Shaw. The man found dead in a bathing machine on Sunday morning."

Mrs Dunn jumped backwards, her hands clutching her chest. "It wasn't me. Honestly. I had nothing to do with it."

She garbled her words as she struggled to breathe. "You must believe me."

"You mean we should believe it wasn't you who killed him?"

"Yes ... I didn't." Her eyes were wide as Eliza studied her.

"Why did you tell us you'd never seen him before?"

Mrs Dunn's cheeks flushed. "Well ... I ... erm..."

"Is it because, in fact, you did recognise him? It may explain why you hastily changed tables with Miss Anderson, to give yourself an alibi should anything happen to him?"

"No. It wasn't like that. He was responsible for my son's death. A child I'd waited years for." She stifled a sob. "He gave him the wrong dose of something for his asthma, but not once did he show an ounce of remorse. When I heard him talking to you about how difficult the patients and parents were in London, I couldn't carry on..."

"So you let Miss Anderson serve him, knowing she'd be a suspect if anything found its way into his drinks?"

"Not at all. I'd no idea he was going to be poisoned."

"You didn't check with her which drink was his when she was serving our table. Or notice when she arranged a drink for him when he was here on his own?"

"No, honestly, I didn't. You can ask her. I didn't go near his drinks. You have to believe me."

"Very well." Eliza scanned her notes. "What about your husband? We know he had dealings with Dr Shaw when he arrived at the hotel."

"He carried his bags ... that's all."

"Are you sure? We'll be speaking to him later..."

"He didn't do anything. He didn't recognise the doctor until I pointed him out. He was upset when he found out, obviously, but he wouldn't have taken his life. Please, don't blame him..."

"I'll need to speak to him first to find out what he has to say for himself." Eliza closed her notebook. "I'll let you know if we pass any of the information on to the police."

Once they were alone, Connie leaned forward to pour the coffee. "That was informative."

"It was. Did you believe her?"

Connie sat back. "I'd say so. That she's not our murderer, at any rate. I'm not sure I can say the same about Mr Dunn. I suspect she knows something more about him."

Eliza nodded. "I agree, but I'd still like to see her handwriting."

"You think she could be behind the letter?"

"It's possible."

"But why, if she didn't kill him?"

"She may have wanted to talk to David, just like the letter said. To get some peace."

"If that's the case, isn't it a bit of a coincidence that someone poisoned him on the same night?"

"Not if it was Mr Dunn who had the arsenic. She may have told him she was going to meet David, but that wasn't enough for him. Knowing he'd be outside at midnight, Mr Dunn could have told his wife not to upset herself and that he'd deal with him. After all, I've not heard anyone say she was either in the foyer or outside the hotel when David was there."

"So she might not know about her husband?"

Eliza shrugged. "It's a theory, nothing more."

"It makes sense, except–" Connie's forehead creased "–if he knew his wife had written the letter, which he must have done for this idea to work, wasn't he putting his wife at risk of being accused of the murder?"

"Hmm." Eliza took a sip of her coffee. "Maybe he hoped to get away with it because, with his wife at home, she'd have an alibi."

"That's clever."

"Indeed, although, if Mr Dunn is our killer, how did he get the poison into the drinks? He shouldn't have been in the bar."

Connie cocked her head to one side. "He took Dr Shaw's bags to his room. Did anyone ever check whether there was any poison up there? In the water jug, perhaps?"

Eliza shook her head. "I doubt it, and I expect the cleaners will have been in and destroyed the evidence by now."

"But we don't know for sure. Should we ask the police to check?"

Eliza groaned. "I know you're right, but I'd rather not tell Inspector Jarvis what we know. Not yet. Shall we talk to Mr Dunn first and if we find out he had the opportunity to poison David in the bar, we needn't bother with the room?"

Eliza was finishing her coffee when Archie and Mr Bell walked tentatively towards them. "Is it safe to come in now?"

"It is. I'm sorry about before, but Mrs Dunn was unlikely to be so open with you both here."

"And did she talk to you without us?" Archie took the seat opposite her.

"She admitted they were Thomas' parents, and that she recognised David when she served us."

"Did Mr Dunn?"

"We've not spoken to him yet, but she said he didn't until she mentioned it to him."

"Are they both suspects?"

Eliza shook her head. "I really can't see her doing it. She overheard David complaining about the parents in London, which is why she stopped serving us."

"So she had no opportunity to add any poison to his drink?"

"That's what it looks like, unless someone's covering for her. I'll check with Miss Anderson, but I've a feeling she's telling the truth."

"So that leaves Mr Dunn."

"It does, and the likelihood of him being our killer increases with every witness we speak to. He starts work at three o'clock, so we'll aim to speak to him before he starts."

"You and Connie?"

"You and Father, too. If he's our killer, I don't want to confront him on our own."

# CHAPTER TWENTY-ONE

M r Dunn was already in the foyer when the four of them returned from their post-dinner stroll, and Eliza checked the clock above the reception desk.

"You're early today, Mr Dunn."

"No point sitting at home when I could help out here. And earn a bit of money into the bargain." He grinned at her. "May I help you?"

"Actually, you can. I wonder if we could have five minutes of your time to answer a few questions."

Mr Dunn stared at Archie and Mr Bell, who were behind her. "Questions?"

Eliza regained his attention. "Some new information has come to light about the death of Dr Shaw, and we'd like to ask you about it."

"H-how can I help?"

"It needn't take long, sir." Archie stepped forward and ushered him towards the lounge, but Mr Dunn took a step backwards.

"I can't go in there. If I'm seen…"

"Ah." Archie looked at Eliza, who glanced around her.

"Where else would you suggest, bearing in mind Mrs Appleton and I aren't allowed into the bar?"

Mr Dunn checked over both shoulders. "How about we go outside to the Italian Garden? Lovely it is in this weather, and we'll be away from prying eyes."

Eliza nodded. "That sounds ideal. Would you lead the way?"

After they wended their way through a maze of corridors, Mr Dunn held open the door to a magnificent space at the back of the hotel. The centrepiece was a bridge over an ornamental lake.

Eliza caught her breath. "How lovely. I don't know how we missed this."

Archie tutted. "You've been rather preoccupied, that's how. Your father and I sat out here when you went to visit Miss Young. There's a rather pleasant seating area on the other side of the bridge. It should be in the shade by now."

Mr Dunn hesitated. "I've not got long. I need to be at the desk by three o'clock."

"And you will be." Eliza feigned a smile as they walked. "This will be your first summer in Brighton, I presume."

"Yes, it is." He accepted the seat Archie offered him before Eliza continued.

"It must have been quite a shock seeing Dr Shaw in the hotel last Saturday."

"Shock? No. Why?"

"A contact of ours in London, a police inspector, told us about your son."

"My..." He turned his head between Eliza and Archie. "What do you mean?"

"We spoke to your wife earlier, and she confirmed that Dr Shaw was in charge of your son's care when he gave him an overdose of a drug for his asthma."

"I-I didn't recognise him when I greeted him. It was Rose. My wife. She said she'd never forget those blue eyes and black hair."

"When did she tell you about him?"

"I-I don't remember." He removed his hat and rubbed a hand over his head. "Once dinner had finished, I suppose, because she'd have been busy before then."

"When Dr Shaw was out?"

"I-I don't know. Was he?"

Eliza took a deep breath. "All right, let's take it slowly. According to your statement, you first came across Dr Shaw when he asked you to take his bags upstairs."

"That's right."

"And when you came back to the foyer, did you see him again?"

"Not until later when he wanted directions to English's restaurant. He said he had a booking there."

Eliza nodded. "He did, and we've already spoken to the lady he was meeting. What about when he came back to the hotel after dinner?"

Lines appeared around his eyes as he squinted into the sun. "I don't think so.

"But you saw him again at midnight?"

"Did I?"

"We have witnesses who say you were outside the hotel talking to someone when Dr Shaw came out of the hotel."

"Ah, yes. It's coming back to me. He didn't look well. I

thought he was drunk, so I left him to it. They're often more trouble than they're worth."

Eliza checked her notebook. "You originally told us you left work at eleven o'clock that evening. Why were you still outside at midnight?"

"I ... erm ... I'd been to the alehouse. I often do..."

"Yet you didn't tell us earlier that you came back, or that you'd seen Dr Shaw."

"No." He released a deep sigh. "If you must know, I guessed I was probably one of the last people to see him alive and didn't want anyone pointing a finger at me."

"But that's exactly what people will do now, given that you lied to us."

"I realise that, but I didn't know what to do. Rose was distraught, seeing the man who'd taken her child from her, so I couldn't admit to seeing him in case the police blamed me for his death."

"What happened when Dr Shaw left the hotel that night?"

He shrugged. "Nothing. I was talking to someone. I couldn't tell you who..."

"We believe he was a stocky man wearing a dark jacket and light-coloured trousers."

"He may have been, but a lot of men walk past the hotel dressed like that."

"But you didn't know him?"

"No. We exchanged a few words, and he carried on his way."

"And once you were alone, did you notice where Dr Shaw went?"

"Erm ... no. I don't think I did. Oh ... wait, yes. He was on his way to the beach. The last time I saw him, he was going down the steps." Mr Dunn checked his pocket watch and jumped to his feet. "I'm sorry, I must go. It's two minutes past..."

Archie raised an eyebrow at Eliza as Mr Dunn disappeared. "What did you make of that?"

She puffed out her cheeks. "I'm not convinced he's telling the truth."

"Me neither." Connie shuddered. "He seemed to struggle to answer each question as if he had to think about it."

Mr Bell grunted. "He didn't mention bringing Dr Shaw into the lounge either when he arrived back from the restaurant."

Eliza gasped. "You didn't tell me that. Why didn't you mention it sooner?"

"I'm sure we did. He brought him into the lounge and got him a brandy."

"You most certainly did not." She stared at Connie. "Did he?"

"I don't remember hearing about it."

Eliza put her hands to her head. "Didn't you think it was important that he served him a drink, given we're looking for someone who added arsenic to one or more of David's? Mr Dunn could easily have added the poison to the brandy."

The two men looked at each other before Archie grimaced.

"I didn't give it much thought. Mr Dunn didn't come to the table. He just showed David where we were and disappeared."

"But he brought him a drink?"

Mr Bell nodded. "He did. Not that he interrupted us. He

put the glass in front of Dr Shaw and left. I suppose that's why we forgot about it."

Connie shifted in her seat. "You even specifically asked him."

"You're right. I did. I'd have asked why he was lying if I'd known... Why didn't either of you question what he said?"

Archie held up his hands. "I'm sorry, but in fairness, he didn't give us chance before he left."

"And we didn't realise it was important. We only found out this morning that Mr Dunn had a motive."

Eliza huffed. "I suppose so. I'll have a word with him again later, but I think we should speak to Mrs Dunn's mother first."

Connie stared at her. "Mrs Dunn's mother?"

"I'm sure it's only a formality, but she has to be a suspect, given the child was her grandson."

"But she wasn't in the hotel at the time Dr Shaw was most likely poisoned."

Eliza creased the side of her cheek. "I'm not sure we can say that until we've spoken to her. She was certainly in the hotel when David arrived, because she was talking to Mrs Dunn. Perhaps she didn't go straight back to her lodgings when she left the lounge."

Archie grunted. "Are you suggesting she'd gone looking for the poison?"

"Why not?"

"Because she's an elderly woman. She wouldn't go to the stores."

"We can't discount her because of that. She may be very fit for her age."

"I doubt it." Mr Bell scowled at his daughter. "Didn't you

see her leave the lounge? It looked like she was walking with a limp."

"I can't say I noticed. We should still speak to her. Even if she's not our killer, she may have seen something."

Connie's forehead creased. "Do we know where she's staying? Or even what her name is?"

Eliza groaned. "No. Mrs Dunn said she was at a guest house on the other side of the Grand Hotel, but I don't know which one."

"Not to worry." Connie's tone was jolly. "We'll have to promenade between here and the corner of the street and see if we can find her."

"Or hope she comes here for afternoon tea. Then we could follow her back to wherever she's staying."

Archie interrupted. "You do realise we go home on Saturday? We've not got time to wait for this woman to show up again. Why don't you ask Mrs Dunn?"

"And give her mother warning that we're looking for her?"

"What else can we do? I'm afraid to say that it's time you talked to the police. We'll have to leave it to them once we go home."

Eliza rested her hands on her cheeks. "And let them take the credit for all our hard work? No. We've still got thirty-six hours in Brighton. We need to identify the killer before we leave."

Mr Bell snorted. "That's if they'll let us leave."

Archie's face reddened. "Of course they will. I'll have a full surgery to deal with on Monday morning."

"As far as I'm aware, the inspector still has you and Eliza down as suspects, and he told us not to leave the hotel until he'd finished his enquiries."

"Then I'll have a word with him." Archie stood up, but Eliza caught hold of his arm.

"Not yet. At the very least, will you wait until tomorrow?"

He stared down at her. "I can't hang around here while he's got nothing better to do than accuse people like us of a murder we didn't commit."

"I know that, but please, let me speak to Mrs Dunn's mother first. She may know something we've missed..."

Archie helped her to her feet. "Very well, but we'll need to tell him what we know straight after breakfast tomorrow. This has gone on for long enough."

## CHAPTER TWENTY-TWO

Eliza and Connie bid farewell to Mr Topham and walked the full length of the portico before they paused and looked to their left.

"There's the Grand Hotel, so Mrs Dunn's mother should be in one of the guest houses on the other side of that."

Connie nodded. "At least she gave us some idea where to find her. Shall we go?"

Eliza linked her arm through Connie's as they set off across the front of the hotel. "I hope she's still in Brighton. I've not seen her in the hotel for a few days."

"We've been out a lot ourselves, so we may have missed her. Do you remember what she looked like? I didn't pay her much attention."

"Not so much her face, but she was a large lady, and her hat was very elaborate with those flowers covering the top."

"Ah, yes. Peonies, weren't they?"

"Something like that. It's to be hoped she didn't bring a different hat for each day of the week."

Connie chuckled. "Let's just look for anyone wearing a fancy hat, then."

They reached the Grand within two minutes of leaving the Metropole and as they strolled past, Eliza pointed to the row of five guest houses beyond.

"Would you say it's one of those?"

"I hope so. If not, we've no idea how far down she might be."

"I'm sure she wouldn't stay too far away. It's a shame the windows are so high. You can't see anything."

"Unless she sits in the window."

"We can live in hope." They walked slowly, peering up at each building, but Eliza sighed when they arrived at the street corner at the end of the block. "There's not much to see."

"We didn't really expect there to be."

"I know, but I'd hoped to be wrong... The best thing to do is turn round and walk back to our hotel. There's still a chance we'll bump into her."

Once they were at the Metropole, Eliza ushered Connie towards the door.

"Are we giving up?"

"Not at all. I just want to check she's not come here for afternoon tea while we were out. If she's not in the lounge, we'll do the walk again."

Eliza's eyes flicked around the foyer as they walked to the lounge entrance. Mrs Dunn met them as they went in.

"You're late this afternoon."

"Oh, we're not stopping." Eliza remembered her smile. "I- I wondered if my husband was in here."

She shook her head. "I can't say I've seen him this afternoon. Shall I pass him a message if he comes in?"

"There's no need, thank you. You must be busy."

Mrs Dunn glanced behind her. "We're not too bad. The rush has been and gone."

"And you've no mother to talk to either?"

Mrs Dunn's cheeks coloured. "Not at the moment, although I'm hoping she'll pay me a visit later. She said she was going to the beach."

"That's nice. We've not been down there yet ... other than to study the bathing machine."

Mrs Dunn's back straightened. "I don't go often myself. If you'll excuse me, I need to be getting on."

Eliza grimaced as she left. "I put my foot in it there."

"You didn't do it on purpose, and at least we know the mother's still in Brighton and hasn't been in today. We could sit and wait here until she does?"

Eliza shook her head. "Mrs Dunn didn't seem certain she'd be calling, and we can't afford to waste any time. I suggest we take another walk. If she turns up here, she should still be around when we come back."

The two of them strolled to the corner of the street and then to the hotel, four times, before they stopped on the street corner and stared at the row of guest houses. The sun was still bright, and Eliza raised a hand to shield her eyes. "I've a feeling we're wasting our shoe leather."

"Is it time to sit in the hotel and hope she comes in?"

"We may have to. Oh ... no. Look ... over there by the steps." Eliza pointed across the road towards the beach. "There's the hat."

Connie followed her gaze. "Are you sure it's her?"

"I think so. She's walking with a limp, too, which matches with what Father said."

"Who are the couple with her? It looks as if she knows them, but I thought she was on her own."

"You and me both, but I've seen them before. In the lounge, if I'm not mistaken, but I've not seen all three of them together. I've not seen the couple talking to Mrs Dunn, either."

"They may have met in the guest house and the couple invited the mother to join them?"

"Perhaps." Eliza's eyes narrowed as she studied them. "Have you noticed how stocky the man is?"

"And what he's wearing." Connie gasped as she stared at Eliza. "It has to be the man we're looking for."

"He certainly matches the description of the one seen talking to Mr Dunn. Their conversation would make sense if the mother knows both of them."

"Mr Dunn said he didn't know who he was talking to."

"He's already lied to us, so it's quite possible he was less than honest about that, too. He may have good reason."

Connie creased her cheek. "If not, they'd better have a good alibi."

They shuffled backwards into the shade of the nearest building, but their eyes remained fixed on the trio as they crossed the road and headed to the guest house furthest from them.

"Will you follow them in?"

Eliza paused. "Not yet. If I'd been on the beach all afternoon, I'd want to go and change before doing anything else."

"They may be eager for a drink."

"They may, but either way, they should still be in there if we come back in a quarter of an hour. It may be better to do that rather than pounce on them as soon as they go in. I think we should try to make this as informal as possible. If they've got anything to hide, they'll remain tight-lipped if we push them too much."

"Whatever we say, they're not likely to admit they've just killed a man."

"No, but it will be what they don't say, as much as what they do. That will be key."

Once the suspects disappeared up the front steps, Eliza and Connie resumed their stroll. Eliza glanced after them into the entrance hall.

"I hope this place serves tea to non-residents. I've built up quite a thirst."

"Wouldn't we be better talking to them at our hotel?"

"We can't guarantee they'll make their way there. Besides–" Eliza pulled her gaze from the door "–I'd rather Mrs Dunn wasn't around. If all those people have been to our hotel, why haven't they been together? Especially if they know each other."

"We don't always go out with Dr Thomson and Mr Bell."

"Maybe not, but we're with them most of the time." She turned to Connie. "Why do I get the impression they've deliberately stayed apart?"

"Do you think they have anything to do with the murder?"

"Nothing would surprise me." Eliza pulled her purse from her handbag and flicked open the catch. "There's not enough in there for two teas. Archie should be in the lounge by now. Let me go and get some money, and hopefully by the time we come back, they'll have had the chance to freshen up."

# CHAPTER TWENTY-THREE

A rchie and Mr Bell were at their usual table by the window when Eliza and Connie arrived at the hotel, and they stood up as the ladies approached.

"About time, too. Have you had afternoon tea?"

"No, we've not had chance, and we can't stay, either." She grinned at him. "We've found out where Mrs Dunn's mother is staying. Not only that, it looks like she isn't on her own. Would you let me have a little money so we can take tea at the guest house she's in?"

Mr Bell retook his seat. "I thought it was strange that she was on her own. Do you know who the other people are?"

Eliza shook her head as Archie placed a half-crown coin into her hand. "Not yet, but we soon will. Hopefully, we'll be here to join you for a pre-dinner drink. We'll see you later."

Connie scurried behind Eliza as she headed out to the foyer. "That won't give us long."

"That's why we're in a hurry. I hope ... this woman ... I wish I knew her name ... I hope she's in the lounge of this guest house when we get there. I don't want to be sitting waiting for her."

"Will we stay for tea if she isn't?"

Eliza's pace slowed. "We'll have to. We might not get another chance."

She took a deep breath as she reached the steps of the guest house and grimaced at Connie before leading the way to the front door. The entrance hall was long and narrow, with a flight of stairs at the far end. A mahogany table, occupied by a middle-aged woman in a dark dress, took up much of the space between the two.

"Good afternoon, ladies. May I help?"

Eliza flashed her best smile. "My companion and I were hoping to get a pot of tea. Would that be possible?"

"Certainly. Walk this way." The woman stood up and led them into a moderately sized front room, overfilled with a selection of worn armchairs arranged around six wooden tables. "Take a seat and I'll bring one for you."

Eliza squeezed through the chairs and headed towards the window, which was framed with a pair of red velvet curtains and a valance edged with golden tassels. She smiled at the group sitting at the next table as she took her seat. "Good afternoon."

Mrs Dunn's mother nodded in acknowledgement while the man and woman, sitting on either side of her, spoke together.

"Good afternoon."

Eliza glanced out of the window. "This is rather nice. Are you staying here?"

Mrs Dunn's mother spoke. "We are. Until Saturday, that is."

"The same as us. It's been a lovely week. Have you travelled far?"

"From London."

"Not dissimilar to us, although we're in a village just outside the city, so we have an extra train journey once we reach Victoria station. I'm Mrs Thomson, by the way, and this is my companion, Mrs Appleton."

"Good afternoon." Connie spoke as the younger couple exchanged glances. After a moment, the man responded.

"Mr and Mrs Craven. And this is my wife's mother, Mrs Price."

Eliza beamed at them. "It's lovely to meet you all. Am I right in thinking I've seen each of you taking afternoon tea in the Metropole?"

Mrs Craven studied the table as her husband replied. "Have you taken tea there yourself?"

"Only when we first arrived. It was lovely, but to be honest, we didn't want our dinner afterwards, so now we make do with a pot of tea."

Mr Craven stared at them. "You're staying at the Metropole?"

"Only for the week."

"Then what are you doing in a place like this?" His cheeks flushed as the lady from the hall arrived with their tea. "As nice as it is."

Eliza waited for the woman to position their tea beside a plate of biscuits and disappear again into the hallway. "Forgive me for not saying earlier, but we've actually come to talk to you."

Mr Craven's mouth fell open and he looked at his

companions before turning back to Eliza. "How do you even know who we are?"

"We didn't until a minute ago, but I've seen Mrs Price in the Metropole, and our waitress at the hotel, Mrs Dunn, happened to mention that Mrs Price is her mother." She looked at Mrs Craven. "I've seen you and your husband in the hotel, too, but I didn't realise you were Mrs Dunn's sister. I've not seen the three of you together before."

"No... It's painful for my sister to spend time with me..." She glanced at her swollen belly. "Besides, Mother likes to be on her own with Rose, so my husband and I don't trouble them."

"Not that it's done any good." Mrs Price tutted. "She should never have moved down here. I told her at the time it was a mistake..."

Eliza studied her. "Mrs Dunn said she was trying to persuade you to move here."

"Tsch! Her and her fanciful ideas. She knows I won't. I've told her enough times I want her in London, and thankfully, now that *monster*'s dead, there's no reason for her not to come with me."

Eliza raised both eyebrows. "Dr Shaw, you mean?"

"Yes, I do. He had no right to be a doctor, the damage he did. Rose was beside herself when he arrived in the hotel. I'm not surprised she had to leave London."

"Did you ever meet him?"

"Never. I couldn't bear the thought of being in the same room as him."

"But you knew who he was?"

"Of course I did ... and the way he treated Rose."

Eliza gulped. "Were you in Brighton on Saturday?"

"We were. We arrived shortly after two o'clock, and as soon as I'd unpacked, I walked to the Metropole to visit Rose. She'd been expecting me, so I didn't want to keep her waiting. Once I left, we had dinner here, and afterwards the three of us sat here until I went up to bed."

"May I ask what time you left the hotel?"

Mrs Price shrugged. "I was sitting here by six o'clock, so shortly before that."

"And you came straight here?"

"Where else would I go?"

"I couldn't say, I'm afraid I don't know Brighton... Were Mr and Mrs Craven waiting for you when you got here?"

"Yes, at this table." She gave an unexpected chuckle. "We seem to have made it our own this week."

Eliza glanced between the Cravens. "Can you confirm the timing?"

Mrs Craven nodded. "I would say so. My husband and I took a walk along the promenade while Mother was with Rose, but we were waiting for her when she got back. We all stayed in the guest house for the rest of the evening until I took Mother up to bed at ten o'clock. I remember the time because the clock sounded as we stood up and I was surprised it was so late."

"Did you go to bed at the same time?"

"No, I helped Mother with the stairs because she rolled her ankle on the beach and didn't want to put any weight on it." She looked at her husband. "Once I came back, the two of us stayed here for another half an hour."

"What about you, Mr Craven? While your wife and Mrs Price were upstairs, did you stay here on your own?"

"Why do you ask? You're beginning to sound like the police."

"No, clearly we're not, but–" she glanced at Connie "–we are *helping them* with their enquiries."

"You're helping the police?"

"We are ... and they asked us to speak to you to save them calling tomorrow."

"Oh ... that's most unusual."

Eliza grimaced. "Unfortunately, we've been involved in several murder enquires over recent years, and the police have got used to us being around."

"I see." His eyes narrowed as he studied them. "If you must know, I waited here for my wife."

"And how long was she gone?"

He shrugged. "I don't recall. Ten minutes, maybe fifteen..."

"Mrs Craven?"

"Erm ... it's hard to say. I'd say it was more like fifteen minutes by the time Mother was settled."

A barman polishing glasses behind a counter in the corner of the room caught Eliza's attention.

"Could he confirm that?"

Mr Craven's eyes darted to the corner of the room. "Y-yes. I think so. Although, no, actually ... I wasn't here for the whole time."

Eliza raised an eyebrow, but allowed him to continue.

"Forgive me for being indelicate, but I needed to use the lavatory ... which I did before my wife returned."

"And the lavatory is ... where?"

"Oh ... erm ... at the back of the hotel. Beyond the stairs."

Eliza looked again at Mrs Craven. "Can you confirm your husband was in his chair when you returned?"

"Yes, he was. I didn't actually realise he'd moved. He'd even ordered me another glass of sherry."

"So you stayed here for another half an hour. Did you go to bed together at that point?"

"No. I went upstairs, but my husband stayed down here."

"Alone?"

Mr Craven shifted in his seat. "I had one last snifter..."

"In this bar?"

"Y-yes..."

"Can anyone confirm that?"

"I couldn't say... Possibly the barman?"

Eliza made a note in her book. "I'll check with the bartender on the way out, but it's curious, because if you were in the guest house, there must be someone else in Brighton who matches your description."

"Someone else?" His voice squeaked as he spoke. "There must be plenty of men who look like me."

"I'm sure you're right. It must be coincidental that one of them was outside the Metropole, talking to Mr Dunn shortly before Dr Shaw was murdered."

Mrs Craven glared at her husband. "Is that why it took you so long to come to bed? I told you..."

"N-no ... I ..." He stood up and paced to the door. "It's not what you think."

"What is it then?" Mrs Price didn't take her eyes from him.

"I only nipped out for five minutes. I wanted a word with Tommy when he'd finished work."

"What was so important that you needed to speak to him at that hour?"

"It was to be a surprise for you and Mother."

"What sort of surprise?"

He ran a finger around his collar. "If I tell you, it will spoil it…"

Mrs Craven paused as her husband returned to the table and took hold of her shoulders.

"Please don't make a scene."

She pursed her lips as he stared down at her. "Very well. We'll speak about it later."

Eliza's eyes flicked between the two of them until Mr Craven retook his seat. "If you don't mind, Mr Craven, I'd still like to speak to you about your meeting with Mr Dunn."

"It was private…"

"In which case, I doubt you'd want me to mention it to the police. They'd like to know who the man was with Mr Dunn, so unless you talk to me, I'll have no option but to suggest they come here to talk to you."

He pulled a ruffled handkerchief from his pocket and wiped his brow. "Very well, I'll speak to you. But not here. I often walk to the Metropole to see Tommy before he starts work. I could meet you there tomorrow…"

"Unfortunately, we don't have the luxury of time. Once we've finished this tea, we're heading back for dinner. Would you be kind enough to escort us? It need only take five minutes." *If you've nothing to hide.*

# CHAPTER TWENTY-FOUR

The sun was falling towards the sea as the three of them left the guest house, and Mr Craven straightened his hat as Eliza walked with Connie to his left.

"I'm sorry to cause friction between you and your wife. She must have been in a deep sleep when you got back to your room."

"She was. Thankfully."

"The extra sherry did the trick, then?"

"What! No, that's not why I bought it for her." He sighed. "The truth is, Tommy had had a trying day and asked me to go to the alehouse with him. My wife doesn't like me going to such places. She thinks they're beneath me."

"You didn't mention you'd seen Mr Dunn earlier in the day."

"Because I hadn't."

"Yet you said he'd had a tiring day. How did you know if you hadn't seen him?"

Mr Craven's cheeks coloured. "I didn't know when I left

the guest house. I just needed some air and walked to the hotel. That's when he suggested it."

"I see. Were Mr Dunn's problems anything to do with the arrival of Dr Shaw?"

"Indirectly. Rose had been very upset to see him, and Tommy had needed to comfort her. On a Saturday of all days. His busiest day."

"Is that why Mrs Price spent so long taking afternoon tea? To keep Mrs Dunn company?"

"I can't answer that, but I imagine Rose was pleased she was there. The two of them like to talk at the best of times. Even on a normal day, Mother can be at the hotel for half the afternoon."

"And Mr Dunn must have been glad he had you as a drinking partner."

"I suppose so, but the way he was, he'd have gone out whether I'd been around or not."

"And what time did you return to the Metropole?" When Mr Craven's gaze turned vacant, Eliza continued. "If you'd like me to jog your memory, we've several witnesses who saw someone matching your description outside the hotel, at around midnight."

"Ah, yes."

"Did you see Dr Shaw leave the hotel?"

"N-no ... how could I? I don't know what he looks like."

"I'm sorry. I assumed you would. He was an attractive man with black hair and blue eyes."

He shrugged. "It was too dark to notice anything like that."

"Perhaps you remember seeing a man who many presumed to be a drunkard, then?"

He bit his lip before answering. "I do, as it happens ... but I didn't know he was a man about to go to his death. If he was drunk, he may have found a bathing machine to go to sleep in and didn't wake up when the tide came in."

Eliza studied the hotel portico as they approached. "I'm sure that's what the killer wants us to believe. Unfortunately, there are several aspects of Dr Shaw's death that suggest something more sinister than that."

"I'm afraid I'm not familiar with the case. We've not discussed it."

Eliza stared at him. "You've not spoken about it?"

"Why would we?"

"The man was murdered!"

"But we didn't know him."

"Mr and Mrs Dunn did! As far as they are concerned, he was responsible for your nephew's death. Don't you care about that?"

Mr Craven kicked at a stone on the ground. "We didn't like to mention it in front of the Dunns. They were upset enough about my wife's condition..."

"So that's not what you were discussing with Mr Dunn? May I ask what he wanted to talk about?"

"Nothing in particular. He wanted company, no more than that." Mr Craven stopped and looked at her. "*I* was the one who wanted to speak to *him*. I'd hoped to persuade him to move back to London. You saw how upset Mrs Price is about them being down here..."

Eliza's eyes narrowed. "Mrs Price suggested they move because Dr Shaw's no longer with us, yet he was still alive when you were with Mr Dunn. Had you had a premonition?"

"No ... of course not... I wanted them to move, anyway. I had no idea he was about to die ... how could I?"

"I was hoping you might tell me."

He blinked several times. "You can't think I killed him?"

"Did you?"

"I didn't know the man."

"But you were aware of the damage he'd done to the family. Had it not been for him, Mr and Mrs Dunn would still be in London."

"I didn't even consider that. I miss them being in Lambeth, too."

"So, when you saw Dr Shaw stumble from the hotel, did you see an opportunity to end his life and hope it would persuade the Dunns to move back to London? Or did you think it would endear you to your mother-in-law?"

Mr Craven snorted. "I've no need to please her. We get on perfectly well."

"Really? She looked less than pleased with you in the guest house."

"Nonsense. She's just in a tetchy mood because Rose won't move."

"So you had no success persuading Mr Dunn?"

Mr Craven huffed as he studied the horizon over the sea. "No."

"All right. Before you go, could you tell me where Dr Shaw went after he left the hotel?"

Mr Craven shrugged. "I wasn't paying attention. I noticed the commotion, but once the fellow reached the road, I bid Tommy good night and went back to the guest house."

"So you left Mr Dunn outside alone?"

"He was about to head in the opposite direction."

"So neither of you has an alibi for the time Dr Shaw most likely died?"

"What time was that?"

"The police can't say for certain, but shortly after midnight at the earliest."

"I was at the guest house by then."

"Can anyone confirm that? You've already said your wife was asleep."

"I ... erm ..." He sighed. "No, actually, they can't. The bar was all locked up and there was no one at the desk."

"Very well. Thank you, Mr Craven. We'll leave it for now, but I may need to contact you tomorrow."

Mr Craven gave a cursory wave as Mr Topham pulled open the hotel door for Eliza and Connie.

"Good evening, ladies. You've been out for a long time."

"A bit too long, Mr Topham. We need a sit-down."

"Well, enjoy your evening."

Eliza lowered her voice as she spoke to Connie. "I'll be ready for that sherry when we get to the lounge."

Connie's face fell as Eliza headed to the porters' desk. "Aren't we going straight there?"

"I'd like to see if I can catch Mr Dunn first."

"Do you think we can trust him? He seems to tell lies more than he tells the truth."

"He does, which has to make him our prime suspect, especially knowing Mr Craven left him alone to walk home. We need to confirm what time he arrived."

"Won't Mrs Dunn be more likely to help with that?"

Eliza nodded. "We'll speak to both of them, but we'll need to find out where they live first so we know when he should have arrived."

"She may have been asleep, too, given he was so late."

"That's true, but if she was as upset by David's presence as everyone says, she may have had difficulty sleeping. Oh—" Eliza's shoulders sagged as she glanced over to the porters' desk "—there's no sign of him. Hopefully, he's just taken someone's bags upstairs. We may as well go and find Archie and then come back."

They strolled into the lounge, but Eliza let out a low groan when there was another couple sitting in their usual seats. "Don't tell me Archie and Father are in the bar. I could do with that sherry."

"No, look, they're over in the far corner." Connie caught hold of her arm and ushered her across the room.

"What are you doing over here?" Eliza flopped into the chair Archie held out for her.

"Colonel and Mrs Giles were here and asked us to join them. You've not long since missed them."

"I can't say I'm sorry."

"Oh dear. Was it that bad?"

"On the contrary, it was better than expected, although I'm not sure it helped."

Connie leaned forward. "The couple with Mrs Price were Mrs Dunn's sister and her husband."

"Mrs Price being Mrs Dunn's mother?"

"Yes." Eliza reached for the glass of sherry waiting for her. "Her and her daughter, Mrs Craven, appear to have an alibi for Saturday after she left here."

"So she didn't go down to the stores for the poison?"

"It doesn't look like it. She admitted she was here in the afternoon, but said she went straight to the guest house when she left, arriving shortly before six o'clock. She stayed there with her daughter and son-in-law until she went to bed at ten. I checked with the barman while we were there, and he confirmed it. Sadly for Mr Craven, he has no such defence for later in the evening. The bar closed as he ordered his last drink and the barman left the lounge before Mr Craven. He did admit he was the man with Mr Dunn when David left the Metropole, but he left him shortly afterwards to go to the guest house. Again, no one was around to confirm what time he got there."

"Not even his wife?"

Eliza shook her head. "She'd already told me, before she realised he'd slipped out, that she was asleep when he got to the room. Something possibly helped by the extra glass of sherry he bought her before bed."

Archie gave a low whistle. "So, he could be our killer?"

"He could, but we've no evidence he was in the hotel when David was poisoned. In fact, the barman at his guest house confirmed he was there, so unless he and Mr Dunn were working together..."

"It's a possibility..." Archie took a sip of sherry. "It would explain a lot."

"It would. The only thing nagging me about it all is that it happened so quickly. Would they have been able to coordinate everything at such short notice? And why do it as soon as he arrived? The Cravens are here until Saturday, so there shouldn't have been any rush."

"They must have had their reasons."

"I'm just not sure we'll be able to find out what they are." Eliza looked at Connie. "Unless you've an idea forming."

Connie shook her head. "Nothing."

"That's a shame."

"It's more than that." Archie held Eliza's gaze. "Tomorrow's our last day. We have to tell the police what we've found and leave the rest to them."

Eliza put her hands to her face. "I feel as if we're so close. Have either of you spoken to the police lately? We could do with finding out where they're up to and see if it matches what we've learned."

"Especially about the letter." Connie picked up her sherry glass. "We need to know if they've ruled us out so we can go home."

Mr Bell nodded. "She has a point."

"All right, but before we involve the police, will you give me enough time to speak to Mr and Mrs Dunn again? I want to check what time Mr Dunn returned home on Saturday night."

"And what will you do with that information?"

Eliza scowled at her husband. "I'm hoping it will give us the proof we need that he's our man. If he didn't get home until one o'clock in the morning or later, he has some explaining to do."

"And what if he was home before quarter past twelve, or if Mrs Dunn was asleep when he got home? Does that mean he's innocent?"

"Not necessarily, but it would suggest he was unlikely to be the one who put David into the bathing machine. If it wasn't him, it has to be Mr Craven. Doesn't it?"

"It sounds reasonable, but you must sort this out, one way or another, by the morning. We can't put off speaking to the police for any longer."

# CHAPTER TWENTY-FIVE

Eliza ran her spoon around her dessert bowl and finished the last mouthful of ice cream at the end of their evening meal. "That was lovely."

Archie emptied his glass of lemonade. "It always is. What would you like to do now?"

"I need to speak to Mr and Mrs Dunn, but I've not seen either of them this evening." Eliza glanced around the dining room. "I hope they've not disappeared."

Connie dabbed her lips with her napkin. "It would suggest Mr Dunn's guilty if they have. Mrs Price or Mr Craven may have spoken to them after we left."

"That would implicate them, too, if they felt it necessary to warn him." Eliza settled back in her seat. "I'll speak to Mr Topham on our way to the lounge and ask if he knows where they are."

Mr Bell put his napkin on the table. "If we're all finished, we may as well go now. We don't have a lot of time."

Archie and Mr Bell assisted the ladies with their chairs before Archie led them into the foyer.

"Would you like us to go for a quick snifter while you're looking for the Dunns?"

Eliza tutted. "We won't be long. You could order a pot of tea for us instead."

"I'll leave that to you. I don't know how long you'll be." He gave a brief wave as they headed towards the bar. "We'll only have one."

Mr Topham was alone by the door as Archie and Mr Bell left, and Eliza approached him with a smile.

"You're quiet tonight."

"It'll pick up soon enough once people finish dinner and go for a final walk of the day. Will you be going out yourselves?"

"Not tonight. We did a lot of walking earlier, so an evening in the lounge is in order. We've just come to ask if you've seen Mr or Mrs Dunn recently?"

He stood up straight and scanned the foyer. "Now you mention it, I don't think I have. Mr Dunn was here earlier, but I couldn't tell you where he disappeared to. You could try the Italian Garden. He often takes his break out there."

"Thank you, we will ... if we can remember the way." Eliza stared towards the right-hand corner of the foyer, but Mr Topham pointed over her shoulder.

"Take the door on the left and follow the corridor straight to the back of the hotel."

Eliza's brow furrowed. "We went through a door on the right last time, and there were more turns than I can remember."

"Yes, you can go that way, but it's much easier taking the left-hand route. Who told you to go the other way?"

"We were with Mr Dunn, and he escorted us."

Mr Topham tutted. "He probably wanted to impress you. He does things like that."

"Well, at least there's an easier way. Thank you, Mr Topham." Eliza linked Connie's arm as they set off across the foyer. "Let's find out what Mr Dunn didn't want us to see."

"What do you mean?"

"We were in the foyer, about to go into the lounge, when he offered to take us into the garden, yet he chose the longest route. Why would he do that?"

"Does it suggest he's guilty?"

"Things weren't looking good for him before today. I'd say he's got even more explaining to do now."

Once they reached the far corner, a gentleman held open the door and they stepped into a long corridor. Connie glanced around her.

"This must be the kitchen area. Could that be why Mr Dunn didn't come this way? Perhaps it's for staff only."

Eliza shook her head. "Mr Topham wouldn't have sent us this way if it was. Besides, it's still nicely decorated. Most staff areas are usually quite stark." She paused as a short corridor branched away to their left. "There's a hatch down there. Could it be the hatch the waitresses use when they order drinks from the bar?"

Connie shrugged. "Why don't we take a look?" She checked over both shoulders, then beckoned Eliza to follow her.

"I'm coming."

They scurried towards the hatch at the end of the corridor, where Eliza bent forward to peep through the opening. "It's the bar. Archie and Father are over by the far wall."

"Let me see." Connie squeezed in beside her. "Where's the barman?"

"That's a good question." Eliza peered into the dimly lit room. "I thought he didn't leave the bar."

"It looks quiet in there. Maybe he's slipped out because he's nothing to do."

Eliza flinched at the sound of footsteps and straightened up as Miss Anderson walked towards them.

"Mrs Thomson. What are you doing here?"

"I ... erm ... we were ... looking for Dr Thomson and wondered if he was in the bar."

"Let me check."

They stood to either side as Miss Anderson thrust her head through the hatch.

"Yes, there he is. Should I get someone to tell him you want a word?"

"Oh, no. Don't trouble him. I just wanted to know where he was. I'm sure he'll join us in the lounge shortly."

"Well, if he doesn't, let me know and I'll ask a waiter to fetch him for you."

"I will." Eliza looked back at the hatch. "You may have a bit of a wait. I didn't see Mr Forshaw at the bar."

"He'll be around somewhere; most likely collecting glasses."

She put a piece of paper on the hatch and tapped a small bell that hung to the side. "I'll leave this here for him. He'll have it ready by the time I get back."

"Do you often leave orders on there?"

"If Mr Forshaw's busy, we do."

"Which is how often?"

Miss Anderson shrugged. "Quite often, especially of an

evening, but he's very reliable. The drinks are always waiting when we bring the next order."

Eliza pursed her lips. "Right, well, thank you for that. We'd better carry on. We're on our way to the Italian Garden."

"Oh, you've not far to go. Just go to the main corridor, turn left and keep walking."

"We will. Thank you."

Eliza and Connie walked to the garden in silence, but once outside, Eliza stopped and stared at her friend.

"Did you see that?"

"What?"

"The way Miss Anderson left the order on the bar. If she does that regularly, anyone could read it..."

"And tamper with the drinks if they were left on the hatch for the waitress."

"Exactly." Eliza's eyes narrowed. "Anyone could have added the poison."

"Assuming they knew who each drink belonged to."

Eliza creased her cheek. "Which leads us back to the question, how did the poisoner know which drinks were for David?"

Dusk was falling as they resumed their stroll towards the bridge in the centre of the garden, and Eliza groaned as they climbed slowly to the highest point.

"My legs are trying to tell me we've done too much walking already today. Still, if either of the Dunns are out here, we should find them."

Connie gazed out across the ornamental lake. "It is a lovely setting. It's a shame we haven't had more time to enjoy it." She pointed towards the left-hand corner of the garden nearest the hotel. "Is that an entrance to the street outside?"

"It looks like it."

"I wasn't expecting that. I thought the garden would only be for hotel guests. Obviously not."

"No..."

Connie wandered to the other side of the bridge. "Oh, look."

"What is it?"

"Mr and Mrs Dunn." She nodded towards the far corner.

"It looks like a serious conversation."

"Do we disturb them?"

Eliza took a deep breath. "No. If we do, we'll have to speak to them together, which I don't want to do. Let's hope one of them goes in before the other and we'll catch the one who stays out here."

They stood admiring the neatly trimmed borders, but didn't wait long before Mr Dunn stood up and strode into the hotel.

Eliza grimaced. "He looks angry."

"And Mrs Dunn is crying. Should we leave her be?"

"I'm afraid we don't have time for that. Perhaps we can offer a sympathetic ear." Eliza led the way down the bridge and turned along the path towards Mrs Dunn. She looked up as they approached.

"Mrs Thomson, Mrs Appleton. What are you doing here?"

"Just taking in the scenery. Are you all right?"

Mrs Dunn wiped her eyes with the back of her hands. "I'm being silly. I'll be fine."

"Nonsense. It's been a difficult week for you. Is there anything we can do to help?"

She shook her head. "Nobody can. Mother wants me to move to London, but Tommy won't hear of it. He says we're settled here and going with her will only bring back memories. I don't want to upset either of them, but I can't be in two places at once."

Eliza sighed. "It's not easy. If you could make your own decision, what would you do?"

"It's difficult. It's nice being in Brighton, but it's not the same..."

"You miss London?"

She nodded. "Tommy doesn't understand, though."

"Perhaps give him time. He may change his mind."

"He won't. He loves it here. That's why he works all the hours God sends."

"So I heard." Eliza bit her lip. "Do you mind me asking what time he got home last Saturday?"

"Saturday? Why?"

"We ... erm ... we need to make sure he has an alibi for the evening Dr Shaw died."

"You don't think he had anything to do with it?"

"We ... can't be sure. That's why we want to check. Was he late?"

"Not that I know. No later than usual, anyway."

"So, what time would that be?"

She shrugged. "Half past twelve, one o'clock. I'm usually in bed."

"He's as late as that?"

"He can be on a Saturday... He likes to go to the alehouse."

"But you can't be certain of the time?"

Her shoulders heaved. "Not precisely, although it was definitely before two. I've not been sleeping terribly well, but when I woke up on Saturday night and checked the clock, I could hear him snoring."

"All right, thank you. Don't let us keep you any longer. When are you due in the lounge?"

She glanced at the clock tower to her left. "I should be there now, but Miss Anderson said she'd cover for me." She stood up. "I shouldn't take advantage of her, though."

Eliza gave her a sympathetic smile. "I hope you sort things out with Mr Dunn."

"He'll be happy as long as we stay in Brighton. I'll see you later."

Eliza watched her leave. "So no one can vouch for Mr Dunn before two o'clock."

"Do you think he's guilty?"

"I do. We just need the evidence to show he put the poison in the drink and everything else will fall into place."

Connie sighed. "We'd better go and find him, then."

# CHAPTER TWENTY-SIX

Mr Dunn was at the porters' desk when they walked back into the foyer, but he didn't smile as they approached.

"Good evening, Mr Dunn. You've been rather elusive today."

"I've been busy."

"Well, I hope we've caught you at a good time. We'd like a word with you."

"It's not convenient at the moment. We're still expecting guests..."

"This won't take long, and I'm afraid it can't wait. We'll be leaving the hotel on Saturday and we'd like to finish our investigation into Dr Shaw's death before we speak to the police."

"The police?" His eyes darted from one to the other. "What do you mean?"

"I'm concerned you've been rather careless with the information you've given us this week, and I'm hoping you can clarify a couple of things for us."

"Careless?"

"I asked you the other day about the interactions you'd had with Dr Shaw, but you failed to mention you saw him when he returned from the restaurant on Saturday evening. Why would that be?"

His cheeks coloured. "I-I must have forgotten."

"And did you forget you showed him to my husband's table ... and then fetched him a glass of brandy?"

He removed his hat and rubbed a hand over his head. "It's been a difficult time... My mind must have gone blank."

"Which is rather convenient, given Dr Shaw was poisoned, presumably by something put into one or more of his drinks?"

Mr Dunn took a step backwards. "I didn't do it."

"Then perhaps you can tell me who poured the drink you delivered to Dr Shaw."

"Mr Forshaw ... I presume."

"You presume?"

He let out a deep sigh. "If you must know, I got my wife to order it for me, but when she came back to the lounge, I took it from her and delivered it myself. Men prefer to be served by men ... when the ladies aren't with them."

"Why didn't you ask a waiter to serve him instead of your wife?"

"They were all busy. Now, if you'll excuse me..."

"Actually, there is something else. You told us the man you were talking to outside the hotel at midnight was a passing stranger. That wasn't true, either, was it?"

He stared at them but said nothing.

"Since we last spoke, we've learned the man in question was your brother-in-law, Mr Craven."

"Ah. Yes. I'd forgotten about him, but there was someone else... I thought you meant him."

"I don't think so." Eliza pursed her lips. "We had a long talk to Mr Craven earlier, and he confirmed the two of you visited the alehouse when you finished work, but you were back here by the time Dr Shaw left the hotel. Is there a reason you lied?"

"No. Of course not, but it's none of your business who I talk to."

Eliza recoiled. "It is when a man who walked past you was found dead hours later. Can you tell us where you were between midnight and two o'clock?"

"I ... I ... I walked home and went to bed."

"And what time did you get home?"

"At a guess, about quarter to one. I left shortly after I saw the doctor, and it takes about half an hour to get home."

"Can anyone confirm that?"

"My wife."

Eliza raised an eyebrow. "Are you sure? Think very carefully, Mr Dunn."

His eyes shifted as he took a sip of the lemonade he had hidden beneath the counter. "Well, she was in bed ... I couldn't say if she heard me come in."

"We happen to know she didn't." She studied him as he scanned the foyer. "You do realise you're the only person we've found who had both the motive and opportunity to murder Dr Shaw?"

"What if I am? I didn't do it."

"We only have your word for it."

"But you don't have any witnesses who saw me poison him or put him in the bathing machine ... because I didn't.

Now, if you'll excuse me, I've other things on my mind at the moment."

Eliza huffed as he stomped to the door. "We'll speak to him again tomorrow. It sounds like he's still upset about his argument with Mrs Dunn."

"He's right about us not having any witnesses, though."

"I know. We'll just have to hope the police have done better than us on that front." Eliza was about to head for the lounge but stopped. "Wait a minute." She pivoted towards the door leading to the garden, leaving Connie to chase after her. "Where are we going?"

Eliza put a finger to her lips and strode into the corridor. Once they were alone, she paused and glanced around. "Is there anywhere we can hide?"

"Who from?"

"Everyone. Don't worry, it shouldn't be for long..." She stopped at the short corridor leading to the serving hatch and popped her head into a room opposite. As soon as she confirmed it was empty, she ushered Connie inside. "This should be perfect, as long as no one comes in."

"What are we doing?"

"I'm hoping Mrs Dunn will arrive with an order and that she'll leave it on the hatch like Miss Anderson did earlier."

"Why? Do you think someone's about to poison another drink?"

"Gosh, I hope not. No, I'm baffled by the letter in David's room and the fact we've still no idea who wrote it. If Mr Dunn's guilty, we need to see Mrs Dunn's handwriting."

"You think the two of them did it together?"

"I don't know, but there has to be a reason Mr Dunn asked

his wife to get David a brandy, rather than there being no waiters available."

"It does seem strange given the number working here."

"And it would confirm that it was no coincidence he was outside the hotel at midnight." Eliza kept her eyes on the corridor opposite and straightened up as Mrs Dunn turned towards the hatch. "That didn't take long."

"Is she here?"

"She is." She cocked her ear to the door. "And there's the bell. Hopefully, we'll be in luck."

She put her head out of the door as Mrs Dunn disappeared and then turned back to Connie. "The coast's clear. Will you stand on the corner opposite and give me a sign if anyone's coming?"

"How do I do that?"

"Just bid them good evening in a loud voice and I'll hear you. Come on, we don't have long."

Eliza scurried the short distance to the hatch while Connie paced across the entrance to the corridor. She'd only just picked up the piece of paper when Connie's shrill voice rang out.

"Good evening. You're late out tonight."

"Mrs Appleton."

Eliza darted behind a section of protruding wall. *Whose voice is that?*

"We were late having dinner and thought we'd come here for a nightcap."

"That's nice. Is it quicker walking through the garden?"

"We happened to be towards the rear of our guest house, so it made sense to use the back door."

*Mr Craven.*

"That's handy."

"Are you on your own?"

Eliza held her breath as Mrs Price's voice echoed down the corridor.

"Oh ... no. My companion, Mrs Thomson, she ... she's looking for her husband and wondered if he was in the bar. We're not allowed in ourselves, so this is a good place to check."

Taking her cue, Eliza ambled towards them. "Mr and Mrs Craven, Mrs Price, what a surprise."

Mrs Price bristled. "I don't know why. We're here to visit my daughter, as we have done on many occasions. We've just left it later tonight in the hope that the lounge would be quieter. There's no point calling if we can't talk."

"Absolutely not. Well, don't let us stop you..."

"Did you find your husband?" Mrs Price fixed her eyes on Eliza.

"My husband?"

"Mrs Appleton said you were looking for him."

"Oh ... that ... erm, no, I didn't see him. Not that you can see the whole bar from the hatch. He may be sitting in a corner. We'll try the lounge again."

Mr Craven stepped backwards and ushered them in front of him. "After you. Mother isn't walking terribly quickly at the moment."

"Ah, thank you. Have a nice evening."

The Cravens and Mrs Price were still hovering in the corridor when Eliza and Connie reached the door to the foyer, and Eliza paused to watch them.

"Mrs Price's ankle must be troubling her tonight."

Connie followed her gaze. "She's clutching Mrs Craven's arm. Perhaps she should let Dr Thomson look at it."

"It can't be that bad or they wouldn't have walked here. She's probably just looking for sympathy." Eliza continued through the door, but stopped as it closed behind them. "Well done for saying I was looking for Archie."

"Did you see the handwriting?"

"I did, but it bore no resemblance to the letter the inspector showed me."

"So, what do we do now?"

"I'm at a loss. I was sure it would be her, given Mr Dunn is almost certainly guilty."

"Maybe he got someone else to write it for him. It may have been too incriminating to ask her, in case anyone found out. She does do a lot of writing in her notebook."

"Would he be likely to share his intentions with anyone else?"

"Maybe he just said he wanted to talk to him...?"

"It's a possibility. Come along, we'd better go and find Archie."

The lounge was busy when they arrived, and they paused in the doorway as they surveyed the room. "Mrs Price won't be best pleased. I doubt Mrs Dunn will have a minute."

Connie glanced behind her. "It will be last orders before they arrive at this rate."

Eliza sniggered but groaned when she noticed Archie waving to them from a table in the far corner. "He's sat with the Gileses."

"And the Brookses and the ladies."

"What do I say? I can't announce the killer before we talk to the police."

Connie faced her as they sauntered to the table. "Tell them what you would have told them two hours ago. That we don't know."

Archie stood up to greet them when they arrived. "It's a good job I didn't order that pot of tea. What kept you?"

"We've been busy." She flashed a smile around the rest of the group. "Good evening, everyone. It looks like you're having quite a party."

Mrs Gardener leaned forward. "We're all keen to hear how your investigation's coming along. Each of us has tried talking to the inspector over the last few days, but he won't tell us anything."

"No, they want to keep their cards close to their chest. Assuming they have any cards." She grinned at Mrs Smith's bemused face. "It may be because they've not much information to share."

"They know a few things." Colonel Giles paused as all eyes turned to him. "I spoke with the inspector this morning. He didn't want to give much away, but said they've finally eliminated the barman, Mr Forshaw, from their enquiries. The arsenic on the bar had convinced them he was involved, but they found none on his clothes and the man has no motive."

"Have they found a motive for anyone else?"

"He wouldn't say, I'm afraid. What about you? Have you discovered anything?"

Eliza bit her lip. *Do I tell them? No.* "Not a lot. We found out that Mr and Mrs Dunn, the waitress and porter, knew the victim from when they lived in London, but it's not much of a motive for murder."

"Had they had a falling-out?"

"They've not said anything..."

"Lies!"

Eliza's cheeks coloured as the colonel banged a hand on the table. "I-I'm sorry."

"Oh, not you. The villain. He has to be dishonest to put you off the scent. There may be more to the Dunns than meets the eye."

"Y-yes. That was our thought, too. We'll speak to them again tomorrow." *Change the subject.* "When you spoke to the police, did they mention whether they'd identified the writer of the letter found in Dr Shaw's room?"

"They've still no idea. I asked straight out, but they said none of the samples they'd taken matched the script of the letter."

"So they've not asked the right person yet."

Colonel Giles's moustache twitched. "Either that, or the culprit forged someone else's handwriting."

"That would be difficult to establish."

Mr Brooks brightened as the colonel's shoulders slumped. "There was one bit of interesting news. They've confirmed that the arsenic found during the post mortem was from the hotel store."

"Oh, splendid. Did they tell you who had access?"

"Most of the male workers, by the sound of it. The room was only locked of an evening, so anyone could have helped themselves."

Eliza puffed out her cheeks. *Not so helpful after all.*

"That's frustrating. What else have they been doing with their time?"

The colonel shook his head. "All they've told us is that they've been interrogating poor Mr Forshaw, taking handwriting samples and looking for the source of the arsenic. If they've done anything else, they're keeping it to themselves."

# CHAPTER TWENTY-SEVEN

A rchie watched Eliza as she poured him a cup of tea early the following morning.

"Are you sure about Mr Dunn? It's quite an accusation when you've no proof."

"I just can't see who else it could be. He had a motive. He was around the bar when David got back to the hotel. He was outside when David went to the beach ... and he had access to the storeroom..."

"There are still unanswered questions, though, such as how did he get the poison into the first drink, who delivered the letter and how did he move the bathing machine down the beach? You can't accuse someone of murder just because we're at the end of our holiday..."

Mr Bell nodded. "Not when he could go to the gallows."

Eliza let out a deep sigh. "I hate it when you're right, but I don't see how anyone else could have done it. Not alone, at any rate."

"We've already discussed the idea of Mr Craven helping him. Doesn't that warrant more investigation? Another thing to consider is that the poisoner didn't actually kill David. It was the person who put him into the bathing machine. He drowned, remember?"

"But the poison meant he was less likely to escape the water. In all probability, it was the same person who did both."

"You can't go off probabilities. The fact is, it wasn't the poison that killed him."

"So you don't want me to say anything to the police?"

"You need to speak to them, but be honest. Give them the information you have, the deductions you've made, and let them find the evidence to support it. We can't do any more with only one day left."

"You're right." She peered around Connie to see into the foyer. "I've not seen them this morning. Has anyone else?"

Archie shook his head. "I've not, but it's still early. Besides, they've been here for the last five days. They've probably spoken to everyone they need to."

"So we'll have to go to the police station?"

"It's looking likely."

Eliza sighed. "Shall we take a walk first? If they're not here by the time we get back, we'll ask Mr Topham for directions."

Archie grinned at Mr Bell. "Actually, we have a better idea. You promised at the start of the week that you'd join us on the beach, yet other than going to look at the bathing machines, you've not been down there once. Why don't we find a quiet spot and discuss everything before we tell the police?"

"Aren't we a bit early to go down there?"

"It's the best time of the day, before the sun gets too warm."

"Very well. As long as you don't expect us to go into the water."

He laughed. "Perish the thought. I'll take that slowly."

The dining room was filling up when they left the table, and as they reached the foyer, Eliza pointed to the doorman.

"He's on his own. I'll ask him for directions now, in case he's busy later."

"We'll join you, seeing we're on our way out."

Eliza smiled as she walked towards the door. "Good morning, Mr Topham. Is everything all right?"

"Mrs Thomson..." His face fell.

"Whatever's the matter?"

He hesitated as he glanced at Archie. "I'm not sure I'm allowed to tell you this, but I must share it with someone. Inspector Jarvis was in earlier to speak to the hotel manager. It's poor Mr Dunn ... he's dead..."

"Dead!" Eliza clamped a hand over her mouth as her eyes widened. "I'm sorry, but what a shock. Do you have any idea what happened? And how?"

"All I was told is that Mrs Dunn woke up sometime during the night, and he wasn't moving ... or snoring. She could tell straight away that something was wrong."

"Oh my goodness, the poor woman!" She shook her head. "This is the closest I've come to being speechless." She turned to Archie. "We won't need directions to the police station any more. Inspector Jarvis isn't likely to be there."

Archie scratched his head. "Mr Topham, do you know if the inspector's still here?"

"No, he arrived early and left about an hour ago. He said

he'd be back."

"Did he say if there was anything suspicious about the death?"

Mr Topham sighed. "He didn't say as such, but I did hear him mention Dr Shaw's death to the manager."

"So they could be linked?"

"I can't be certain, but it did cross my mind."

"Thank you, Mr Topham, and our condolences. It must be quite a shock."

"It certainly is, madam." He held open the door. "Perhaps a walk will help you."

"I'm sure it will, but what about you? Will you be all right?"

"I'll manage. I'd rather not go too far from the hotel in case they want to talk to me."

"Of course. Will you have much to tell them?"

"Only that Mr Dunn left the hotel shortly after eleven last night, and when I asked if he was on his way to the alehouse, he said he hadn't been feeling himself, so was going straight home."

Eliza gasped. "Did he have a stomach ache?"

"He didn't say, but I know he'd had words with Mrs Dunn earlier in the evening and so I put it down to that."

"You're right." *Don't jump to conclusions.* "We saw them together in the garden. She must feel terrible..."

"At least she has her family down here to take care of her."

"Indeed. Well, thank you again, Mr Topham. I need to go somewhere quiet and think about this."

The four of them crossed the road in silence and carried on to the steps leading to the beach. Eliza stood at the top and studied the pebbles below.

"Must we?"

"Yes, we must." Archie urged her to keep walking. "We'll find some deckchairs and sit down. You've had a shock."

"I'll say." She gazed up at her husband. "Is there any chance he got the message wrong?"

"It didn't look like it. He looked as bewildered as you."

Connie took Eliza's arm as they reached the beach. "Does that change things with Dr Shaw's death, or do you still think he did it?"

Eliza sighed. "I don't know what to think any more."

"Perhaps someone knew he was our killer and wanted revenge?"

Eliza's eyes shot open. "Miss Young, you mean?"

Connie shrugged. "I suppose so, given she's the only one down here who knew him."

"Apart from us." Archie grimaced. "Unless we're certain Miss Young is involved, it would be tricky discussing it with the police without getting ourselves into more trouble."

"That's a good point." Eliza bit her lip. "Another option might be that Mr Dunn found out who killed Dr Shaw, and the killer wanted to silence him before he told anyone."

Archie blew out his cheeks. "It's impossible to say at this stage without knowing more about the cause of death…"

Eliza studied him. "Would you be able to find out?"

"You know the inspector won't talk to us."

"Not from him. You'd need to speak to Dr Poole. I wonder if he's done the post mortem yet."

"I doubt it if they only found the body a few hours ago."

"Would you ask him, anyway? The cause of death may be obvious enough for them to hazard a guess."

"Let's sit down and think about things first. I don't want to go asking questions, only for you to come up with a whole lot more when I come back." He found a group of four deckchairs and helped Eliza into hers as Mr Bell assisted Connie. "Comfortable?"

Eliza glanced down at the wooden frame holding the striped canvas seat in position. "More than I expected. Not that I've any idea how I'll get out of it again."

Mr Bell laughed. "We'll have to leave you there, then."

Eliza grimaced. "It's no laughing matter."

"No, and neither is Mr Dunn." Archie took the deckchair between Eliza and Mr Bell. "How was he last night when you spoke to him?"

"I'd agree with Mr Topham. He was a bit out of sorts because of his argument with Mrs Dunn, but he became rather sheepish when we pointed out he'd lied to us."

Connie nodded. "He looked angry when he left the garden after talking to his wife."

Archie raised an eyebrow. "Do you know what they argued about?"

"We do, as it happens. It was about whether to stay in Brighton or move back to London. Apparently, he wanted to stay, but she wants to leave."

"I presume it hadn't been resolved."

Eliza shook her head. "It hadn't been when we saw her. She was terribly upset."

"Upset enough to want to kill her husband?"

Eliza shuddered. "I'd hope not. It's a rather trivial reason."

"In isolation, perhaps, but she was upset after the death of her son, so seeing David may have been too much for her..."

"Possibly."

Connie gasped. "What if they had more words when Mr Dunn was at home and it got out of hand?"

Eliza held her gaze. "How would she have killed him, though? He was a lot bigger than her."

Mr Bell interrupted. "Poison again?"

"If it was Mrs Dunn ... and it was when he got home from work ... she wouldn't have had time to poison him. Not with arsenic, anyway." Eliza turned back to Connie. "I'm beginning to think the person who killed Mr Dunn is the same person who killed David."

"You thought Mr Dunn was the killer."

"I did, but as Archie pointed out, there were still things we hadn't worked out. Perhaps we were wrong."

Connie sank into her chair. "You're not usually."

"No, but this investigation hasn't been usual. First, no one seemed to have a motive, then there was no evidence. Now it feels like everyone is lying..."

"So we're back to square one?"

"Not necessarily. Let me think..." Eliza rested her head on the back of the deckchair, her eyes half-closed to shield them from the morning sun, but she sat up again when the dippers arrived to open up the bathing machines. Several middle-aged women with ample bosoms and full skirts attended to those nearest them.

"At least Mr Dunn wasn't in one of those. It's still a mystery how David ended up in a machine halfway down the beach." She watched as they untied the ropes holding them close to the wall, but suddenly sat up with a start. "Did you see that?"

Connie looked at her. "What?"

"The bathing machine closest to us. When she untied the

217

rope, it moved by itself until the woman put a stick under the wheel." Eliza struggled to get out of the chair, but pushed herself to her feet before Archie could help her.

"Where are you going?"

"To speak to the dipper." She headed straight for the woman in charge, remembering her smile as she approached. "Good morning."

The woman stared at her, and then at Archie as he joined them. "You're too early if you want to go into the water."

"Oh gracious, I don't want to do that. I was just watching you and noticed you using a stick to stop the machine rolling."

"What of it?"

"I-I was wondering how far down the beach would it go if you took the stick away."

The woman glanced along the length of the beach. "To the line where the pebbles flatten. Why?"

"So a woman could move the bathing machine as far as the plateau on her own."

"I do..."

"Yes ... right. You don't need one of your colleagues to help?"

"Not on this part of the beach. We do lower down ... or when we're coming back."

Eliza scanned the beach. "That's very helpful. Thank you." She grabbed Archie's arm as they hurried back to Connie and Mr Bell. "Did you hear that? A woman could have moved the machine to the position it was in when they found David."

Archie stared at her. "You can't think Mrs Dunn did it?"

"Whether I do or not isn't the point right now. The fact is, she *could* have done."

# CHAPTER TWENTY-EIGHT

Inspector Jarvis was in the foyer when Mr Topham opened the door to let them into the Metropole. Not that he appeared to notice them. Eliza studied the manager he was talking to as they headed to the lounge.

"It must be time for elevenses."

Archie checked his pocket watch. "To the minute."

They entered the room as Colonel Giles waved to Archie.

"It's not like him to be in at this hour."

Eliza grinned. "He won't want to miss anything. I wonder if the police have spoken to any guests yet."

"I would say we're about to find out."

"Dr Thomson. Please join us. We were hoping you'd be here."

Archie shook his hand. "We've been down to the beach, but morning coffee beckoned."

"Well, I'm very glad it did. We've just ordered." He lowered his voice as Eliza and Connie took their seats. "What can you tell us about this porter? Found dead, I heard."

Eliza nodded. "That's about all the police are telling people. Have they spoken to you about it yet?"

"No. They're speaking to the staff first, but they'd better hurry up. Most of us go home tomorrow and we can't be waiting for them to get around to us."

"You're right. We'd hoped to speak to them about Dr Shaw's death, but they won't be worried about that today." Eliza smiled as Miss Anderson joined them.

"Good morning, all." The waitress looked as if she'd been crying, and Eliza gave her a sympathetic smile.

"Are you all right?"

"I will be. I just can't believe what's happened to Mr Dunn. He was such a nice man ... and Mrs Dunn's bound to leave the hotel now."

Eliza's forehead creased. "You've spoken to her?"

"I don't need to. Mr Dunn was the only reason she was here."

"Has anyone seen her today?"

"Not that I'm aware, but I noticed her mother and sister hurrying past earlier. I imagine they were going to the house."

Connie shook her head. "What an end to their holiday!"

"Yes..." Eliza paused as her eyes flicked to Connie, then Miss Anderson. "Was Mr Craven with them?"

"I didn't see him..."

*Where is he then?*

Miss Anderson glanced around. "I don't mean to be rude, but are you ready to order? I need to get a move on with Mrs Dunn being absent."

Archie grimaced. "I'm sorry, yes. Four coffees, please, and a plate of biscuits."

The colonel leaned over to Eliza as Miss Anderson wrote

out their order. "Is there a reason you wanted to speak to the police about Dr Shaw?"

"Not really, but with us going home tomorrow, we decided we should share our information with them."

"They ought to have worked it out themselves by now. I just hope this latest death doesn't get in the way. I'd like to find out myself who the blighter is who disturbed our holiday."

Eliza grimaced. "We'll need to check *The Times* for that when we get home. I can't see them working it out by tomorrow morning. I'm not even sure they've worked out the motive yet."

"And you have?"

"Oh..."

"You have, haven't you!" He slapped a hand on his thigh. "I knew you would. What is it? A jealous husband?"

Eliza's cheeks coloured. "No, nothing like that. We just found out that the Dunns and Dr Shaw had a falling-out when they were in London, and I'm guessing the Dunns thought the doctor had come to Brighton out of spite."

"And had he?"

"Not at all..."

"But you think Mr Dunn killed your doctor friend?"

Eliza hesitated. "It was a possibility, but not one we'd confirmed. The police will have to follow it up now."

"What about that chap Mr Dunn was talking to outside the hotel?"

Eliza stared at him. "How did you know about him?"

He indicated to Mrs Smith. "The ladies told us. They said they'd seen him in the hotel last night, too. Any idea who he is?"

"Mr Dunn's brother-in-law, Mr Craven..." Eliza suddenly turned to Connie. "We need to go."

"Where to?"

"Down the road." Eliza jumped to her feet. "Excuse us, Colonel. I'll explain later. And to you..." She smiled at Archie as he watched them leave.

"What about coffee?"

"We'll have to hope it's still warm when we get back. I don't expect we'll be long."

Eliza acknowledged Mr Topham as he pulled open the door, but didn't stop until they reached the footpath. "We need to speak to Mr Craven. If he's still around."

"What do you mean?"

She took a deep breath. "I'm worried he's disappeared."

"Why?"

"Because he's got to be the chief suspect now."

"Based on what?"

"Several things. First, we now know he can come into the hotel through the back door, so the fact Mr Topham and the other doorman didn't see him on the night David died means nothing."

"So he could have poisoned Dr Shaw?"

"Exactly." Eliza nodded. "He could have easily slipped into the hotel bar to poison David's drink, or even used the hatch if he saw Miss Anderson with the order. We also know he was in the hotel last night, so he could have poisoned Mr Dunn, as well."

"But we don't know that Mr Dunn *was* poisoned, yet."

"Maybe not, but I'd wager he was. Come along. We need to get to the guest house and hope we can find him."

The desk in the hall was unoccupied when they stepped

through the front door, and Eliza popped her head into the lounge. "Empty."

"What do we do now?"

Eliza wandered to the desk and checked the keys on the rack beside it. "It looks like most of the guests are out."

"It's a shame we don't know which room the Cravens are in."

"We do. Number seven." She smiled as Connie gasped. "I noticed their key on the table when we were here the other day."

"Number seven isn't there."

"Which suggests that if Mrs Craven and Mrs Price are out, Mr Craven should still be here. Come along." Eliza had a foot on the first step of the stairs as Connie scurried around the desk.

"What are you doing?"

"Going to talk to Mr Craven. There's a chance he's still in his room."

"We can't call on a gentleman like that."

Eliza sighed. "Not under normal circumstances, but this is a murder investigation and we go home tomorrow. We don't have a lot of choice."

"Well, don't go into the bedroom..."

"My dear Connie, I'm not that daft."

"But you can get carried away..."

Eliza rolled her eyes and climbed two flights of stairs as directed by the signs. "He'd better be up here after all that."

They wandered along the corridor to room seven and Eliza rapped on the door before putting her ear to the wood. "I can't hear anything..." A second later she jumped backwards as the door opened and Mr Craven stood before them, his shirt unfastened at the neck and his braces hanging loose by his sides.

"Oh, Mr Craven." Her cheeks coloured at his state of undress. "I'm sorry to disturb you, but I'd hoped we could have a word."

He glanced down at his trousers before pulling his braces over his shoulders and reaching for his jacket. "Forgive me. Let me find my tie."

"Please, don't trouble yourself. There really is no need."

He hesitated in the doorway, but reached for it anyway. "What may I do for you?"

"We'd like to ask you about Mr Dunn. Can you tell us anything about his death?"

"No more than the police have told me." His fingers worked quickly as he tied a Windsor knot. "Rose couldn't wake him, and the doctor pronounced him dead when he arrived."

"Did they say what he died of?"

"Not directly but they said there were no visible signs of death, so they suspect poisoning."

*I knew it!* Eliza kept her voice steady. "May I ask when you last saw him?"

"Me! I didn't do it." His eyes widened. "He was my friend."

"Please, Mr Craven, I'm not saying you did, but it would help to know who was the last to see him, and find out how he was."

"Oh. Right. Well, for the record, I met him in the foyer last night when we called at the Metropole."

"Did you stay and talk to him?"

"For a short while. He wasn't busy, so I stayed until some guests arrived."

"What time would that have been?"

"Shortly after we saw you. When was that? About nine o'clock?"

"Sometime around then. How was he when you spoke to him?"

Mr Craven paused. "He wasn't very talkative, to be honest, which I thought was strange at the time, but I put it down to him being angry."

"With Mrs Dunn?"

"Not so much with her as her mother and my wife. He blamed them for unsettling her."

"Did he speak to them about it?"

"I doubt it. He wouldn't want to upset Rose. He just moaned to me instead."

"What did you do once you left him?"

"I came back here ... the barman can vouch for me this time. I didn't want to sit with my mother-in-law. She was in one of her moods."

"And you didn't see him again?"

"No. Mother said they were perfectly capable of walking on their own, and Tommy wasn't in the mood to go to the alehouse. I assumed he was worried he'd upset Rose, and that he wanted to talk to her."

"It sounds as if he was concerned about her."

"He always was ... even more so after young Thomas died."

"And did she feel the same way about him?"

"She did. That's why they moved here, to get away from

everything. I think last night was one of the few times I heard that they'd argued."

"So you don't think there's any chance that Mrs Dunn would have slipped the poison into his drink?"

"Gracious no. It's a preposterous idea."

Eliza sighed. "Do you have any thoughts on who might have wanted him dead?"

He shook his head. "I'm sorry, I don't. He's going to leave a big hole in the family, and Rose must be inconsolable, knowing they had a row last night. And so soon after the boy..."

Eliza glanced at Connie. "I'm sure she will. Please send our condolences when you see her."

He nodded and stepped back, placing a hand on the door. "Will that be all?"

"Actually, there's one more thing." Eliza studied him. "Now he's no longer with us, would you be able to tell us if Mr Dunn was involved in Dr Shaw's death?"

"Of course he wasn't." Mr Craven gawked at them. "How could you even think that?"

"He had the motive and the opportunity to take Dr Shaw's life."

"But he didn't kill him ... he wouldn't."

"You know that?"

"I'd swear my life on it."

"And it wasn't you?"

"No! Why would I hurt a man I'd never met?"

"But he was responsible for your nephew's death."

"That doesn't mean I'd harm him."

"No. All right. Thank you, Mr Craven." Eliza turned to

leave, but Mr Craven hesitated. "Is there something you'd like to tell us?"

He huffed. "I don't know if it's significant, but now Tommy's not here, there's one thing I may as well tell you..."

"What's that?"

"When we were on our way back from the alehouse on Saturday night, he asked me to go to the beach to help him move a bathing machine..."

Eliza's mouth fell open. "It was you!"

"It seemed a strange thing to do, but he said one of the guests had promised to give him half-a-crown to move a machine so they could go for a midnight dip ... away from prying eyes. We'd no idea it would cause any problems ... he was only doing his job."

"Then why didn't he tell us?"

"Because after the doctor died, he realised it looked bad, and he didn't want to incriminate himself ... or me."

"But if he'd told us who asked him to move it, we could have helped him." Eliza sighed. "Did he tell you who it was?"

Mr Craven shook his head. "I'm afraid he didn't. He just said it wouldn't take a minute."

*Typical!* "What happened once it was moved?"

"Nothing. He said the guest didn't need any assistance, so we walked back to the hotel, said our goodbyes and went our separate ways."

"How can you be sure it wasn't Mr Dunn who followed Dr Shaw down to the beach and put him in the machine?"

"Because he told me. When I found out what had happened, I asked him outright if that was why he'd wanted the thing moving. He was horrified by what had happened and denied it immediately. He also made me promise not to say a word to anyone. He didn't want to risk being a suspect."

"And you believed him?"

"I did. You can instinctively tell when someone's telling the truth."

Eliza nodded. "Yes, you can. Well, thank you, Mr Craven. That's been very helpful. If you remember anything else, you know where to find us."

# CHAPTER TWENTY-NINE

The coffee was cold by the time Eliza and Connie returned to the hotel lounge, and Eliza waved to Miss Anderson and asked for another pot. Her seat next to the colonel was still empty, and he patted it as an invitation for her to sit down.

"Do you have anything to tell us?"

She smiled. "Only that it was neither Mr Dunn nor Mr Craven who poisoned our friend."

His shoulders dropped. "Who was it then?"

"I'm afraid we've not worked that out, but we're running out of suspects who knew Dr Shaw well enough to want him dead... Oh..." *No, we're not!* Her head spun to Connie. "We need to go."

"Again! What about coffee?"

"It will have to wait." She looked at the colonel. "Please help yourself to another cup when it arrives. I've a feeling I'll have some news for you when I get back."

Connie trotted beside Eliza as they headed for the foyer. "Where are we going now?"

"To speak to Inspector Jarvis."

Connie stopped and caught her arm. "What on earth for?"

"I think I know who killed David and Mr Dunn."

"Both of them?"

Eliza tried to suppress a grin as she nodded. "I just need the police to confirm a few things."

"Who was it?"

"Actually..." Eliza glanced around her. "Let's go out to the garden and I'll lay out my thinking so you can make sure I've not missed anything. I don't want Inspector Jarvis spotting any flaws..."

The inspector was in the lounge talking to Miss Anderson when they returned, and Eliza stood to one side until he saw her.

"Can't you see I'm busy?"

"I can, but I'd like to talk to you if you can spare five minutes."

"I'll get around to speaking to you in my own good time..."

"So you don't want help finding the murderer?"

The inspector glared at her and concluded his conversation with Miss Anderson before he pulled himself up to his full height. "How many times do I have to tell you to leave this investigation to me?"

"I'm afraid I couldn't do that after you accused me of poisoning my husband's friend. Besides–" Eliza forced an apologetic smile. "–we'd like to go home tomorrow, and it would be nice to see the case resolved before we leave."

"I don't recall giving you permission to leave."

"I'm sure you will once you've heard what we have to say. I believe we've identified your killer."

His dark eyes bored into her. "Which one?"

"Oh, there is only one."

"We have two corpses."

"Both killed by the same person. That bit wasn't difficult to work out once the motive became clear."

"You've found a motive?"

Eliza nodded. "Two, actually, but they're connected. The only thing is, I need you to confirm several things, and there's a key piece of evidence I suspect is still outstanding."

"So you've no proof for your theory."

"Not yet, but I'm hoping you can provide it so we can all have the weekend off."

His upper lip twitched as she held his gaze until, finally, he flinched. "Very well. What do you need to know?"

"Could we go somewhere a little less public? I doubt you'll want anyone overhearing."

He gave a cursory nod and ushered them to a corridor on the right. "Take the first door on the left. There's a table and several chairs. I'll ask the constable to join me."

Eliza and Connie were already seated by the time the two men arrived, and the constable stood by the door as the inspector took a seat on the opposite side of the table.

"Are you going to tell me what this is all about?"

"All in good time, but I wonder if you could help me first. You suggested that Mr Dunn didn't die of natural causes. Do you know how he did die?"

"Dr Poole will do the post mortem this afternoon, but we suspect poisoning. His body was in a similar position to Dr Shaw's."

"So, arsenic, then. I heard you identified traces of rat poison on the bar and it came from the hotel store."

"You shouldn't know that ... but yes, it did."

"Could you tell us precisely where on the bar you found it?"

The inspector's eyes flicked between them. "As ladies are not allowed in the bar, I doubt the exact position would make any difference to you."

"Ah, that's where you'd be wrong. The waitresses have a legitimate reason to use the bar, and so to make life easier for them, there's a hatch at the back that they can access from a corridor on the other side of the wall. Is that where you found the poison?"

"How could you know that? We've not told anyone."

"You helped us, if I'm being honest."

"I did?" A smile flickered across his lips. "Well, yes, that's my job."

"You pointed out that poison is a woman's method of killing, but for a woman to add poison to a drink in the bar, they must have done it through the hatch..."

"Men can use poison, too."

"I'm aware of that, but they'd be more likely to do it in the bar."

"You think one of the waitresses did it?"

"I can't rule it out, but with your help I believe we can eliminate them from the enquiry."

"How?"

"The other piece of information that has so far eluded us is the handwriting on the note found in Dr Shaw's room. Did you ever find a match?"

The inspector huffed. "No. We've checked all the women who came into contact with the doctor, but found nothing."

"What about the waitresses?"

"They both gave a sample of their writing yesterday."

"And you're certain you contacted all the women who knew Dr Shaw?"

"As many as we could find, not that there were many of them."

"No, there weren't, but at a guess I'd say there are more than you think." Eliza glanced at the constable. "Would your man here be able to provide me with a list of the people you've taken handwriting samples from?"

"Why would I agree to that?"

"Because there's a chance the killer isn't on that list and I'd like to check."

"Why don't you tell me who you suspect, and I'll check? I'm not in the habit of giving confidential information to a woman."

Eliza rolled her eyes as she reached into her handbag for a pencil and some paper. "Very well." She jotted the names on the paper and handed it to him.

"Are these guests of the hotel?"

"Not resident guests, but they use the lounge for afternoon tea."

"Who are they? And how do you know about them?"

"I've been doing my research and, as it happens, I'm on rather good terms with an inspector at Scotland Yard. When I was puzzling about a motive, I wrote and asked him for help."

The inspector's face reddened. "You brought in someone from Scotland Yard over my head?"

"Not exactly, I just had a question I thought he'd be able to help with. And he did."

"Did he come to Brighton?"

"Gracious, no. He's far too busy for that. I received a telegram from him. Here." She rummaged in her bag for the piece of paper. "Once I had this, these ladies became known to me. I believe you'll currently find them with Mrs Dunn."

The inspector's mouth fell open as he read the brief note. "Why didn't you tell me about this sooner?"

"If you remember, you were rather scathing about my desire to assist you. I can take a hint…"

"But knowing this would have saved so much time."

Connie sat up straight. "Then you should have listened to Sergeant Cooper. He told you we'd be able to help."

The inspector squeezed his eyes tight. "All right. Point taken. Does Mrs Dunn know these women or are they likely to be a danger to her?"

"I very much doubt they'll harm her. One is her mother and the other her sister. Would you be so kind as to pay them a visit and bring a handwriting sample back for each of them? On the assumption I'm right about the person who wrote the note, I'll explain why they killed our victims."

# CHAPTER THIRTY

Inspector Jarvis looked up from the notes on the table with what Eliza assumed was reluctant admiration.

"So it looks like she's our killer."

"I would say so. Did she take a lot of persuading to do the handwriting sample?"

He nodded. "I had to threaten her with arrest."

"That can only strengthen our case against her. Shall we get everyone together so we can take them through the evidence?"

"Everyone?"

"Not the whole hotel, obviously, but there are people who've helped with the investigation who would be interested to hear the verdict."

"And who would you suggest?"

Eliza smiled. "Would you gather Mrs Dunn, the Cravens, Mrs Price, Miss Young, Miss Anderson, Mr Forshaw and Mr Topham? I'll bring the rest."

"The rest!" He glared at her. "It will be like a circus ... even if I can get a room big enough."

"Please, Inspector. Just think of your weekend off … and the accolades you'll get."

"Very well, if it means you go home and leave me in peace. I'll send word about where we'll hold the meeting shortly."

Two hours later, Eliza grinned at Colonel and Mrs Giles as they entered a cosy lounge near the centre of the hotel with the Brookses and the ladies. There were about a dozen armchairs around the edges of the room and a large settee in front of the fire, on which Mr and Mrs Craven, Mrs Dunn and her mother were already seated.

Archie and Mr Bell stood at the back and, as the seats filled up, Connie took the last chair, beside Mrs Smith and Mrs Gardener.

Eliza wandered over to them. "I hope you're sitting comfortably."

"Oh, yes." Mrs Gardener's eyes sparkled through her pince-nez. "What a splendid way to end the week. Not that our friend was pleased. She'd arranged an afternoon of bridge for us, but we can do that anytime."

Eliza smirked at Connie as she straightened up and headed to the front of the room, where Inspector Jarvis pulled her to one side.

"Do they all need to be here?"

"Of course they do. People appreciate being included..." She scanned the room. "I think that's everyone."

He grunted before clapping his hands together. "Ladies and gentlemen, if I may have your attention." The room fell silent as he ran his gaze around them. "I'm sure when you all began your holiday, you couldn't have imagined it would be marred by the events of this week. One murder would have been bad enough, let alone two, but that, I'm afraid, is what we've faced. As you're aware, we've taken statements from each of you, and I'm grateful to Mrs Thomson and her companion, Mrs Appleton, who provided the final pieces of evidence to allow me to make sense of what happened."

Eliza glared at him.

"Or should I say, allowed *us* to make sense of what happened? Now, where to start...?"

Eliza interrupted. "Perhaps we should begin with the story of Dr Shaw. As most of you know, he was an old friend of my husband's from when they were at medical school. By association, I was acquainted with him, too.

"What we didn't realise was that Dr Shaw also knew Mr and Mrs Dunn. Unfortunately for them, their prior meeting was at St Thomas's Hospital in Lambeth, where Dr Shaw specialised in children's medicine. Towards the end of 1903, he admitted a young boy to his ward for a severe asthma attack. Sadly, he gave him an overdose of the drug he needed to help his breathing, which resulted in his death. That boy was Mr and Mrs Dunn's only child."

Mrs Dunn wiped her eyes with a handkerchief as gasps sounded around the room and people acknowledged the news with their partners.

"If I may continue." Eliza waited for quiet. "As you can imagine, the Dunns were incredibly upset and, with memories of their son all around them in London, they decided to move to Brighton and start a new life. It all appeared to be going well until last Saturday, when two things happened. First, Mrs Dunn's mother, Mrs Price, paid a visit to the Metropole at the start of her holiday, and second, Dr Shaw arrived at the hotel."

Mrs Price stared straight ahead of her into the fire, giving no hint of emotion as she spoke. "My being here had no bearing on the matter."

"Ah, but that's where you're wrong. The truth is that Mrs Price was taking afternoon tea in the lounge when Dr Shaw arrived and joined our table. Mrs Dunn recognised him instantly and fell into something of a panic. Once she'd taken his order, she immediately went to her mother's table to report the turn of events. Later, when she had a spare minute, she also alerted Mr Dunn to Dr Shaw's arrival.

"What the three of them couldn't know was why Dr Shaw was in the hotel or, more crucially, how long he was staying. That was why our killer needed to work quickly, before Dr Shaw disappeared again."

Miss Young's mouth fell open. "So they poisoned him, just like that, without finding out why he was here? All he wanted to do was speak to them and tell them how sorry he was."

"Sadly, our killer wasn't interested in that. Were you, Mrs Price?"

"Don't look at me. I had nothing to do with it."

Eliza tutted. "Come now, you know that isn't true, although you had us fooled for quite some time."

Inspector Jarvis took over. "We believe that Dr Shaw was killed by two doses of white arsenic that were added to his drinks. The first was a vermouth cocktail he finished at around a quarter past six, while the second was in a glass of brandy he ordered when he got back to the hotel after his evening out. Nowadays, it's not easy to find white arsenic, but we learned there was an amount of rat poison in the hotel stores that contained that very ingredient. Guests wouldn't realise it was there, but the staff would know. I imagine Mr Dunn would have been only too happy to share the location of the poison with family members if he needed to."

Mrs Price's face remained impassive. "He was the one who went downstairs for it, but he tried to keep me quiet when I found out."

Eliza studied her. "That turn of events did cross my mind when we heard where the poison had come from, but it was Saturday afternoon, the hotel's busiest day, and Mr Topham confirmed that Mr Dunn wouldn't have had time to go missing for ten or even five minutes. That means someone else must have gone for it. Someone else who knew it was kept in the basement."

"What about the bartender? He mixed the drinks..."

"Don't you start." Mr Forshaw's face reddened. "The police have been on my back for days and found nothing..."

"Well, how did I get to the storeroom with this?" Mrs Price turned to face him, raising a walking stick in her right hand. "I could hardly go down the stairs unnoticed, certainly not quickly."

"Oh!" Eliza paused as Mrs Price turned her gaze back to the front. *When did she get that?* "Your ankle's no better, then? Perhaps my husband can take a look at it for you." Eliza glanced over to Archie, but Mrs Price rolled her shoulders.

"I'm sure there's no need. I've managed well enough so far, and the pain's easing."

"It would be no trouble. I should have asked him to look at it sooner. It may have saved some time. But not to worry..." She pursed her lips as she paced back to the fireplace. "Before

I involve my husband I'd like to go back to the poisoning of Dr Shaw. On that first evening of our holiday, I came down to the lounge with my family to find Dr Shaw sitting alone having a pre-dinner drink at the table we'd used earlier that afternoon. Miss Anderson had served him..."

"I didn't kill him..." The waitress's eyes were wide. "Why would I?"

"We're not saying you did. On the contrary, I believe you were an innocent participant in all this. We didn't realise at the time that the hotel doesn't allow waitresses into the bar, but we've since learned that there's a hatch at the back, which is accessed from a corridor directly connected to the garden. Waitresses fulfil their orders that way, sometimes leaving them on the counter, until Mr Forshaw has time to prepare them. We believe that when Miss Anderson took Dr Shaw's order, she did exactly that, and left it for Mr Forshaw while she returned to the lounge. While this was going on, the poisoner would have had ample opportunity to watch Miss Anderson's movements, and once the drink had been prepared and placed on the hatch, it would only have taken a few seconds for them to slip the arsenic into the drink and disappear out of the hotel through the garden."

Mr Topham straightened his back. "That's how I missed them. I didn't realise outsiders used that door."

"No, indeed." Eliza turned to Mr Craven. "A little tip Mr Dunn put you onto, I presume."

Mr Craven's cheeks coloured. "He said it would save prying eyes if I wanted to speak to him."

"Which seemed to pay off until you mentioned it to your wife and mother-in-law. As it was, last Saturday afternoon, Miss Anderson returned to the hatch several minutes after she'd left the order and unwittingly took the now lethal drink to Dr Shaw."

Miss Anderson gasped. "It's true, I didn't know..." She turned and stared at those behind her. "I didn't..."

Inspector Jarvis interrupted. "We're aware of that, Miss."

"Yes, indeed." Eliza cleared her throat. "So, returning to Dr Shaw. Shortly after he'd finished his drink, he left the hotel to go for dinner, but he became ill as the evening wore on. He managed to act normally, but the problem was, our killer wasn't an expert on poisons. I believe they expected Dr Shaw to be dead before he returned to the hotel, but when he strolled into the foyer nearly four hours later, clearly alive, there was confusion. Had they not put enough arsenic into the cocktail? That was when the killer realised they had to try again. Isn't that right, Mrs Price?"

The older woman glared at her. "Don't ask me. I wasn't here."

Eliza held her gaze. "No, how silly of me, you were in the guest house. You told me you'd gone upstairs at ten o'clock and that your daughter had gone with you because you needed help with the stairs. Presumably that was due to your bad ankle. The thing is, there would be no need for her to help, because I suspect that when my husband examines your ankle, he'll find it perfectly healthy."

"Nonsense. Why else would I use a stick?"

"My guess is to throw us off your scent. I think we'll find that you need that stick about as much as I do."

"Poppycock..."

"Is it really? Could you remind us again how you hurt your leg?"

241

"I rolled my ankle when I was on the beach, if you must know."

"Ah, yes, that's right. Your daughter told us she'd helped you up the stairs that first evening, but there's a slight problem with your story." Eliza paused until she had Mrs Price's attention. "You didn't go to the beach that first afternoon. According to your alibi, you were so keen to see Mrs Dunn, you came straight to the Metropole after you'd unpacked your bags. By your own admission, you then stayed in the hotel until just before six, when you left and walked straight back to your guest house. You then spent the rest of the evening with your other daughter and son-in-law."

Mr Craven looked up. "That's right. When did you go to the beach?"

Eliza smirked at Mrs Price. "That's for her to answer, but whenever it was, I doubt she rolled her ankle. When my companion and I were looking for you on Thursday afternoon, the limp was minimal, as it was when you walked to the hotel last night ... until you saw us."

"It was still painful."

"Then can you explain how you managed to rush to Mrs Dunn's house this morning without any sign of discomfort?"

"What?"

Eliza nodded as Mrs Craven stared at her mother.

"You were seen this morning hurrying past the hotel. Hardly the actions of someone who needs a stick."

"I shouldn't have done that. I thought it was better, but I aggravated it..."

"Are you sure?" Eliza raised an eyebrow. "I would suggest that your sore ankle was nothing more than a sham to give you an alibi. I would even suggest that you deceived your own family to make it look more realistic."

Mr Craven spun to face her. "She did. She was perfectly fine when we arrived in Brighton, but by the time she wanted to go to bed, she could barely walk. Neither my wife nor I saw her damage it."

"Thank you, Mr Craven. That's very helpful. It also supports what I believe is more likely to have happened."

# CHAPTER THIRTY-ONE

The eyes of everyone in the room followed Eliza as she paced across the front of the fireplace before she turned to face Mrs Price.

"I must admit, Mrs Price, your deception almost had us believing that poor Mr Dunn was our murderer, but we now know it was you all along."

Mrs Price said nothing as she stared into her lap.

"I put it to you, Mrs Price, that rather than going to bed at ten o'clock on Saturday night, as you told me, you needed to check on the wellbeing of Dr Shaw. You and your daughter sneaked out the back of the guest house and slipped into the Metropole via the Italian Garden. Mr Craven must have followed you some minutes later, when he'd used the lavatory."

"No!" Mr Craven was on his feet. "That's not right. I admit I did go out, but it was to speak to Tommy about going to the alehouse. I didn't see them in the Metropole."

Mrs Dunn glared at her mother and sister. "I had no idea you were there, either. I thought I saw Mother in the corridor, but I was in such a hurry, I decided I'd imagined it."

"You didn't see me, because I wasn't with her." Mrs Craven looked at her mother. "You asked me to go upstairs to get you a clean handkerchief while you used the lavatory. I thought you were in there for a long time..."

Eliza cocked her head to one side. "Why would she need a clean handkerchief if she was on her way to bed?"

Mrs Craven's mouth opened and closed. "I-I don't know. I didn't ask."

"You never do." Mr Craven spoke through gritted teeth. "You always do whatever she tells you. Just like everyone else ... except Tommy."

"It's what she expects..."

Eliza fixed her eyes on Mrs Price. "So you deceived your daughter and slipped out alone? Not the sort of thing someone with a swollen ankle would usually do. You must have been in something of a panic when you got to the hotel and saw Dr Shaw stroll into the foyer..."

"The only person who would have panicked was Tommy."

"Mam!" Mrs Dunn gasped. "Don't blame him when he isn't here to defend himself. He wouldn't do such a thing."

"Although, he did lie to us, on more than one occasion. For example, it took days for him to admit he met Dr Shaw when he got back from the restaurant, and that he offered to get him a brandy. A brandy he served but asked you to order. Why would he do that when he could have gone into the bar for it himself?"

Mrs Dunn gulped. "He told me he couldn't be seen in the bar and needed to get back to his desk..."

"Then why did he wait for you to collect the drink, then serve it to Dr Shaw himself?"

Mrs Dunn squeezed her eyes tight. "I don't know. He was always looking for extra work, so I thought he was being helpful."

"And you don't believe he'd harm Dr Shaw?"

"No. He was a caring man. He wouldn't hurt anyone."

"Yet your mother seems keen to blame him." Eliza turned back to Mrs Price. "Assuming you saw Mr Dunn take the order, why did you tell him to pass it to his wife?"

Mrs Price spat out her words. "It was *her* job, not his."

"To serve male guests? I'd have thought that was a waiter's job."

Mrs Dunn's mouth fell open, but no words came out as Eliza continued.

"I would say it's much more likely that you needed that order to be fulfilled through the hatch, and not in the bar, where you were prevented from entering. That way, the drink was likely to sit on the hatch where you could add the arsenic before your daughter came back for it."

Mrs Dunn gasped at her mother. "Did you add poison to the drink?"

When Mrs Price failed to reply, Inspector Jarvis continued.

"I'm afraid she did. Your mother had already given Dr Shaw one dose that had apparently not worked, and she needed to get more arsenic into him before she went back to her guest house. Despite her success, she worried that wouldn't work either, and so she came up with the idea of the letter. My guess is that she wrote asking Dr Shaw to meet her outside the hotel at midnight so she could check whether he was alive or not. If he didn't arrive, she would take it as a sign that he was dying, but if he did turn up, she needed another plan."

"I don't know what you're talking about."

"I think you do." Eliza paced in a small circle until she stopped in front of Mrs Price. "Is that when you brought Mr Dunn into your plan? Not that you told him what you were up to. By my estimates, you must have handed Mr Dunn the letter shortly after Dr Shaw got back to the hotel, and told him to deliver it to his room. You then asked him to move the bathing machine on the pretext that you wanted to take a midnight swim. You even offered him half-a-crown in return. Was that to keep him quiet? Or to incriminate him?"

"I'm saying nothing."

"I must say, it was rather clever, and almost had me fooled. I wrongly assumed a woman wouldn't be able to move the box on her own and so I concentrated on the men, but I was wrong on two counts. One, a woman of your stature could have moved it partway down the beach, and two, you didn't actually move it yourself."

"You've no proof of this."

"Ah, but we have." Eliza smiled at Inspector Jarvis as he produced the sample of handwriting from one pocket and the original letter from another. "You put up quite a fight when the inspector asked to see your handwriting, you even tried to alter your script, but looking at the two documents together, it's clear that the writing that was copied was written by the same person who wrote the original."

Inspector Jarvis held the two side by side for his audience to see.

"Just because I wrote a letter, doesn't make me a killer."

"No. And even if you'd poisoned Dr Shaw and done no more, you still wouldn't be, because it wasn't the arsenic that killed him. Not directly, at any rate."

Miss Young looked up, tears filling her eyes. "What do you mean?"

Eliza gave a gentle smile. "Dr Shaw was last seen leaving the hotel around midnight, presumably to meet the person who'd written the letter. Because of the arsenic, he was behaving erratically, but it's safe to say he was very much alive. If he'd received medical care in time, he may well have survived. Unfortunately, most people thought he was drunk, so nobody stepped forward to offer such help. According to Mr Craven, who was one of those who saw him, Dr Shaw continued down to the beach, but when he got there, his killer was waiting for him. He didn't recognise her, as she'd refused to go to the hospital after the child had died, but when she saw him she offered to help."

Mrs Price snarled at her. "I wouldn't help him."

"No, I don't doubt that, but you ushered him into a bathing machine, the one you'd had moved far enough down the beach to meet the incoming tide. Did he assume you were a dipper when you promised it would allow him to take the water and feel better?"

Mrs Price stared defiantly into the fire.

"I imagine he did, which would suit you. You must have imagined that when Dr Shaw's body was discovered, the dippers would more than likely be the key suspects. But there were inconsistencies. The first question I had, was why didn't Dr Shaw wake up when the waves reached him? Any normal person, even if they were asleep, would have been disturbed by a covering of cold water, but he didn't move. That was what first alerted me to the poison. There had to be a reason he stayed where he was."

Miss Young dabbed her tears with a handkerchief. "So that was it. This woman tried to poison him, and when it didn't work, she enticed him into a bathing machine?"

"I did no such thing. It could just as easily have been him." She pointed at Mr Craven.

"Don't blame me. I left Tommy and walked straight to the guest house."

"It must have been Tommy, then."

"Mrs Price. Please." Eliza gasped. "We know Mr Dunn was on his way home by the time of the murder."

Mrs Dunn looked up, her eyes red. "You do?"

Eliza nodded. "We do now. The problem was, your husband had worked out what your mother had done, and that was probably what got him killed."

"But why?"

"Will you tell her, Mrs Price?"

Mrs Dunn gasped as she jumped to her feet. "You killed my Tommy? How could you?"

Mrs Price's face suddenly cracked, and she bowed her head over her knees. "I did it for you. I wanted you home..."

Eliza grimaced. "She believed the only reason you left London was because of Dr Shaw and so if she could just get rid of him, you'd return to London with her..."

Miss Young nearly choked as she glared at Mrs Price. "He wasn't even going back to London. If you'd just spoken to him, you'd have known he planned to stay in Brighton for good. There was no need to kill him."

Eliza nodded. "She's right. What you did on the spur of the moment was quite despicable, but it didn't end there. She hoped that Dr Shaw's death would be enough to persuade you to go back to London with her, but she hadn't bargained for the fact that Mr Dunn didn't want to leave."

"Mam?" Mrs Dunn's eyes widened. "Is this true? I know you said you'd kill Dr Shaw for what he'd done, but I didn't think you meant it."

Eliza sighed. "I'm afraid it is, but once he was dead, Mr Dunn's obstinance meant she had to keep going. She was determined to have her own way and decided that you wouldn't stay in Brighton by yourself. Mr Dunn's fate was sealed, however, when I believe he started blackmailing her." She turned to Mrs Price. "Did he threaten to tell your daughter what you'd done if you didn't leave her alone? Or was he going to go to the police? Either way, you could no longer trust him with your secret and he had to go."

Mrs Craven had sat in silence, but she finally turned to her mother. "After all I've done for you. I've spent my life trying to please you, but it was always Rose you wanted. I was never good enough. Neither was George." She winced as she reached for her husband's hand. "There'll be another grandchild soon, but you'll never meet them. And for what?" She stood up and looked at her husband. "We need to go. I can't bear to be here a moment longer. Inspector, if you want us, you know where we are. Until tomorrow, at least."

Mrs Dunn chased after her sister. "Don't leave me. I never meant to upset you. She turned you against me."

Mrs Craven studied her before she took her arm. "You're right, it wasn't your fault. We'll need each other more than ever now."

"May I come with you? We can talk…"

Mrs Craven nodded, and as the sisters left the room,

escorted by Mr Craven, Eliza took a deep breath and watched Inspector Jarvis put chains on Mrs Price's wrists.

"Well done, Inspector. Do you have all you need from me?"

He smiled across at her. "I do for now, but I'll call back at the hotel later, once Mrs Price is in the cells."

Eliza nodded. "I'm sorry it came to this, Mrs Price, really I am."

# CHAPTER THIRTY-TWO

The tables at the far end of the lounge were busy when Eliza walked in on Archie's arm, but Colonel Giles beckoned them over.

"We've reserved a table for you."

Eliza smiled at the group as she took a seat. "Thank you. You were all obviously quicker with your dinner than we were."

Mrs Smith leaned forward. "We wanted to make sure we were here on time. We didn't want to miss anything."

"Miss anything?"

"We want to hear how you did it!"

"Didn't I explain when we were in the other room?"

Mrs Gardener tutted. "Don't be so modest. You told us what you found out, but you didn't tell us how you did it. We've all been as interested in this case as you, but none of us would have guessed it was this Mrs Price. We didn't even know who she was."

"Ah, I see. It really is just a matter of keeping your eyes and ears open and not jumping to conclusions."

"But *we* all did that…"

Connie smirked at her. "We did have a bit of help … from Inspector Adams."

"Yes, we did. We also had the advantage of knowing Dr Shaw."

Mr Brooks raised an eyebrow. "So, what did this inspector tell you?"

"Well, we knew Dr Shaw had been working at St Thomas's Hospital and, by chance, Mrs Dunn told us they had once lived in Lambeth. The significance of it didn't occur to me until we could find no motive for Dr Shaw's death in Brighton. I sent a telegram to Scotland Yard, and the inspector was the one who told me about the child dying. Once we found out about that, it opened up the rest of the options."

"But how did you even know Mrs Price existed? And the couple with her. They weren't staying at the hotel."

"Mrs Price had been to the hotel for afternoon tea a couple of times, and on one occasion, Mrs Dunn mentioned she was her mother. Once I learned about the death of the child, her grandchild, we had to speak to her."

"And Mrs Dunn just told you where she was staying?"

Eliza chuckled as she looked at Connie. "Not exactly. She'd told us she was in a guest house on the other side of the Grand Hotel. We had no idea which one, but we didn't want to ask in case Mrs Dunn warned her."

Connie grinned. "We walked from the hotel, past the guest houses, to the next corner about five times, until we finally saw her coming back from the beach, with the couple who turned out to be her daughter and son-in-law. We'd no idea they existed either until we saw them together."

Mrs Brooks's eyes were wide. "Did you just approach them?"

Eliza laughed. "No, that would have been far too forward, even for me. We waited for them to go inside and get settled, then we went to the guest house for a cup of tea. We were well in need of one by then, I can tell you."

"I imagine you were."

"It was worth it, though." Connie gave her friend an affectionate look. "Mrs Thomson is so good at talking to strangers that within five minutes we'd found out who they all were and told them why we'd called to see them."

"Not that they told us the truth. It took a lot of questioning before we worked it out."

Mrs Gardener's forehead creased as she leaned forward. "Why are you on telegram-sending terms with an inspector from Scotland Yard?"

It was Archie's turn to laugh. "My wife has always had a passion for solving murders. It started with reports in the newspapers, but when a man turned up on our doorstep one morning and promptly passed away, she embarked on becoming a real-life detective. The police didn't stand a chance."

Eliza scowled at him. "That's not fair. I've helped them out many times, as well you know..."

Mrs Brooks gasped. "So you've done this more than once?"

"Unfortunately, I have. I often seem to be around when a murder takes place."

Mr Bell shook his head. "Half the time, nobody would suspect it was murder if it wasn't for you. Even in Dr Shaw's case. If it hadn't been for you, the police would have put it down as a drunken man, falling asleep in a bathing machine and dying accidentally when the tide came in."

Eliza grinned at him. "It's a good job I was here, then."

Mrs Giles shook her head. "I don't know how you do it ... but well done. We can all sleep peacefully in our beds tonight."

"We can." Eliza smiled at the group. "Are you all packed and ready to leave?"

"We are." Mrs Smith spoke for her and her sister-in-law. "We're leaving on the ten o'clock train. What about everyone else? Will we see you?"

Mr Brooks took the tickets from the inside pocket of his jacket. "The same as us, so we may well be travelling together."

"You won't see us, I'm afraid." Colonel Giles patted his wife's hand. "We're staying for another week to get over the excitement."

Connie gasped. "How lovely."

"I certainly hope so."

"I'd hoped to do that, too." Mr Bell gave Archie a sideways glance. "Given I've hardly seen anything of my daughter and Mrs Appleton this week, I thought it would be rather nice, but Dr Thomson needs to get back to work. Having said that, I've extended our stay by one night."

Eliza's eyes widened. "We're staying until Sunday?"

"I wanted it to be a surprise, but I hope we can spend some time together tomorrow."

"That will be nice." Eliza noticed Connie was suddenly studying the table. "We may need to send a message to Sergeant Cooper. He was going to meet us at the railway station."

Mr Bell grinned at her. "I was going to tell you later, but I've already contacted him. He'll be here at ten o'clock tomorrow morning."

Connie's head jerked up. "He's coming here?"

Mr Bell's face fell. "I thought you'd be pleased."

"Of course she is." Eliza nudged Connie, whose cheeks burned red. "She's just mortified you've mentioned it in front of everyone."

"Ah. My apologies."

"There's no need. That's very kind of you." Connie put her hands on her cheeks. "When did you invite him?"

"Yesterday. He says he's looking forward to it."

Connie gulped. "Will he stay until Sunday?"

"I offered to book him a room, but he was undecided. I suppose we'll find out tomorrow if he brings an overnight bag."

Connie's mouth fell open as Eliza leaned over to her. "And if this doesn't speed things up between the two of you, I'll have to resort to banging your heads together!"

THE NEXT BOOK IN THE SERIES

### *Murder at the Marquee*

*August 1905:* Recently arrived home from their trip to Brighton, Eliza and Connie are preparing for the summer village fete. All is going smoothly until a body is discovered at the back of the marquee.

Can Eliza help the police with their enquiries when Inspector Adams clearly has something more troubling on his mind...?

Visit www.vlmcbeath.com to get your copy.

**More *Eliza Thomson Investigates* coming soon...**

Keep up to date with what's new, by joining the *Eliza Thomson Investigates* newsletter.

Sign up by visiting www.vlmcbeath.com and get your FREE copy of
*A Deadly Tonic*

**Will you leave a review?**

If you enjoyed *Death by the Sea*, I'd be grateful if you'd leave a review.

As well as helping the books gain visibility, letting me know you enjoy them will indicate you'd like more books in the series.

To leave a review, visit your local Amazon store, search for *Death by the Sea,* and scroll down to the review section.

My only plea. Please no spoilers!

∽

*Eliza Thomson Investigates***:**
A historical murder mysteries series:
*A Deadly Tonic* (A Novella)
*Murder in Moreton*
*Death of an Honourable Gent*
*Dying for a Garden Party*
*A Scottish Fling*
*The Palace Murder*
Death by the Sea
Murder at the Marquee
*A Christmas Murder* (A Novella)

## AUTHOR'S NOTE AND ACKNOWLEDGEMENTS

By the late Victorian- and Edwardian-eras, the idea of taking trips to the seaside had become fashionable in England, especially for the well-to-do, and so I thought a week in Brighton, on the south coast of England, would make an ideal backdrop for Eliza's latest escapade.

The rise in the number of people spending time at the seaside had begun in the late eighteenth century, when several prominent doctors suggested that drinking seawater and sea-bathing were good for people's health.

Brighton's proximity to London, and the opening of the London to Brighton railway line in 1840, undoubtedly helped its transformation from fishing village to popular resort, but it was distinguished from its near neighbours by the patronage of the Prince of Wales, later the Prince Regent, in the early nineteenth century.

One of the most impressive hotels of the Victorian-era was the Grand hotel, but in 1890 the Metropole was opened to great fanfare, supplanting the Grand as the resort's most prestigious hotel. This was clearly the venue I had to have for Eliza's holiday.

The early days of sea-bathing brought the problem of needing to disrobe to get the benefits of the water, and many (particularly women) were reluctant to be dressed immodestly in public. The solution came in the form of bathing machines.

Both men and women could change in the privacy of the machine before the whole thing was pulled into the sea. There its occupants would descend into the water away from the gaze of the opposite sex (in addition, beaches were often segregated). Dippers were on hand to help, and would often push people's head under the waves so they gained the most benefit (hence the name, I presume).

As an aside, I would have loved an image of a bathing machine on the cover for the book, but unfortunately, I couldn't find any photographs that would have been suitable.

By the start of the story, in 1905, the use of bathing machines was waning as people became more used to going into the water, but they still persisted, particularly for women, who didn't want to walk from the static beach huts that were replacing them.

I'm always looking for novel ways for people to be murdered in my books (I hope my internet search history is never checked too thoroughly!) and so I thought these machines would make an interesting centrepiece for the story. Of course, that led to the problem of how you would entice someone into the bathing machine and keep them there long enough for them to drown. That's why I needed to introduce the arsenic!

Anyway, that's enough from me! I hope you enjoyed your trip to the seaside, and you're ready to move on to Eliza's next challenge when she and Connie assist at the Moreton-on-Thames summer fete.

Before I go, I'd like to thank my friend Rachel, and husband Stuart for their support with this book and for giving early feedback. I would also like to thank my editor Susan Cunningham, and those people on my Advanced Review Team who gave me comments prior to the book being available. I really appreciate the help of each one of them.

Until next time, take care...

Val

# ALSO BY VL MCBEATH

**Historical Family Sagas Inspired by Family History...**

## The *Ambition & Destiny* Series

### The full series:

Short Story Prequel: *Condemned by Fate*

Part 1: *Hooks & Eyes*

Part 2: *Less Than Equals*

Part 3: *When Time Runs Out*

Part 4: *Only One Winner*

Part 5: *Different World*

A standalone novel: *The Young Widow*

## The *Windsor Street Family Saga*

### The full series:

Part 1: *The Sailor's Promise*

*(an introductory novella)*

Part 2: *The Wife's Dilemma*

Part 3: *The Stewardess's Journey*

Part 4: *The Captain's Order*

Part 5: *The Companion's Secret*

Part 6: *The Mother's Confession*

Part 7: *The Daughter's Defiance*

To find out more about VL McBeath's Family Saga's visit her website at:

**https://www.valmcbeath.com/**

FOLLOW ME

at:

**Website:**
https://valmcbeath.com

**Facebook:**
https://www.facebook.com/VLMcBeath

**BookBub:**
https://www.bookbub.com/authors/vl-mcbeath

Printed in Great Britain
by Amazon